How to Marry a Major

A B.A.D. Guide

Tina Holland

Dedication

For my husband, Major Ken, parts of his personality inspired Myles.

Acknowledgements

First I need to thank all my Writing Groups – Writer Zen Garden, Moorhead Friends Writing Group, Romance Writers Club, & BisMan Writers Guild.

Special thanks to The Romance Writers Club for their Brainstorming Sessions and the Ahh Haa Moment I had regarding this story.

Thanks to Sandra Sookoo for her editing eye and explaining Titles and Entailments so I finally got it.

Thanks to the Word Weavers – Maddy Barone, Renae, Patti & Laura for all their Critiques. Special thanks to M.A. Deppe for her in-depth proofreading after I pivoted this story.

Thanks to Melody Simmons for this wonderful cover art. I appreciate all your hard work.

Last, but certainly not least, thank you to My Readers. I wouldn't be able to keep doing this job I love without you. I hope you enjoy this novel.

Prologue

April 15, 1815
Eastpark Parsonage one mile from Pittham Hall

"I have to leave my home?" Charlotte was so startled by the words of Pelegrina Bullock, the Marchioness of Pittham, that she couldn't think to object. Not that Lady Pittham would have allowed such protests. Charlotte had never liked her late husband's benefactor, but she had not realized the woman was so heartless.

"Reverend Wold has been dead for over a week now. Which is the exact amount of time I believe you have overstayed." With a wave of her hand, Lady Pittham dismissed Charlotte's words. The statuesque woman's girth pushed the startled Charlotte aside as she barged into the cottage.

What little confidence Charlotte possessed vanished.

Lady Pittham's man of business, Mr. John Trotter, trailed behind her like a little dog searching for scraps. With quill and paper, he began to catalog items within the home. Whether to ascertain an article's value or to ensure she didn't steal from his mistress, she didn't know.

"Where shall I go?" She didn't expect an answer from Lady Pittham, but the woman gave her opinion regardless.

"Your destination will be your own, but to indulge your whims, I will allow you the use of my carriage for a day. Tomorrow to be exact." Lady Pittham stopped, her eyebrows cinching tight.

Was the woman smiling? Her face was nothing but teeth, and her nose crinkled as if she was smelling a chamber pot.

"I have to be gone by tomorrow?" Where could she possibly travel in a day?

"Yes, and Mr. Trotter is making note of the cottage items, so be certain to take only what you need." Lady Pittham might have as well said 'and leave the valuables here, regardless of their ownership.'

"Of course." Charlotte resigned herself to fate. This cottage was no longer her home, and she didn't wish to remain.

Lady Pittham released a long audible breath, breaking Charlotte's musings. "Mr. Trotter and I will leave you to finish your packing. The carriage will be here at dawn. If you miss it, you will have to walk to Maplebury and take the mail coach."

Once her ladyship had closed the cottage door, Charlotte immediately packed in earnest. She was not one to mourn life's circumstances. She imagined she should be sad, but she felt nothing. Her life here was over long before Robert died. Lacking the love of Maplebury village or the respect of the marchioness, what did it matter where she found her next home?

As she laid out her black wardrobe for tomorrow's unknown destination, her stomach grumbled. She prepared some weak tea from yesterday's soggy tea leaves and ate the last of her now-stale bread. She went back to packing when a piece of stark white paper caught her eye. Snatching the paper, she unfolded it.

My dearest Charlotte,

I'd like to say I am sorry to hear of your loss, but in truth, perhaps this is for the best. It is not as if there was any love lost between you and the departed Reverend Wold. I know you will resist and consider it charity, but I would dearly like you to come to stay at Devonhold as we celebrate James's birthday the week of April 17th. Consider it an overdue and well-deserved holiday. You are always welcome at our estate.

Yours truly,

Amelia Fitzwilliam

Charlotte stared at the invitation.

When she first received Amelia's missive following Robert's funeral, she disregarded traveling to the Earl of Devonhold's estate and forgot to respond as she fell into the mundane chores of her established routine. Her daily regimen was safer than moving on. Now, she held the forgotten letter like a pauper with a found coin. Would Amelia mind if she simply showed up?

Charlotte shook her head. Her childhood friend wouldn't care if Charlotte arrived unannounced. And what choice did she have? She would go tomorrow with a plan, even if the days to follow were a mystery.

The following morning, Charlotte was promptly on the step before the sun rose. She pulled her pelisse tighter to block the chilling wind. Though winter had started to fade, the wind was a reminder that the season hadn't quite exited.

She probably shouldn't have bothered with the bonnet, either, as the ribbons whipped against her neck; however, if she hadn't, she was certain her hair would have been a mess.

The crunch of wheels on gravel roused her from her thoughts just as the sun peeked over the horizon. Dust curled behind the carriage as it rattled along the drive. She took a step backward, closer to the cottage to prevent dirt from collecting on her belongings and herself.

The coach stopped short, and Charlotte stared at the antique from the last century, being pulled not by four horses but only two. The Pittham crest was invisible unless the light caught the outline just so. The door opened and Charlotte heard Mr. Trotter's supercilious voice before his foot even touched the ground. "Her Ladyship insisted I see you off and inventory the cottage following your leave."

Unsure what to say Charlotte merely nodded. She gathered up her meager yet treasured belongings when a hand touched her shoulder.

"I can see to your items, Mrs. Wold," the driver said.

"Thank you, Thomas," she replied.

Mr. Trotter looked at her belongings. "I'll have to inventory these as well."

Charlotte stepped in front of him. "No, you will not. I will not have you opening my trunk or valise and airing my apparel in the wind for all to see." She was determined to maintain some level of dignity.

"Her ladyship --"

"Does not own my undergarments, nor my gifts prior to my marriage. You and her ladyship may be assured I left every item acquired after my wedding in that wretched, god-forsaken cottage." Charlotte spat on the ground next to the door. She could not leave this place soon enough.

"Reverend Wold was a man of God!" Mr. Trotter stuttered, red in the face.

"By all means then, consider his things which I've left behind sacred relics!" She turned and allowed Thomas to assist her into the carriage. The leather was cracked and springs were poking up between the seats. If she hadn't already been wearing grey, her clothes would've turned the color of dust. She sat in the exact spot outlined by Mr. Trotter, given it was free of dust and the leather appeared intact. The carpet was worn through, and even the upper hinge on the door was misaligned. At least she was leaving this place behind her.

It was too much to hope all would go smoothly. About three hours into the uncomfortable journey the well-worn carriage broke a wheel, and Charlotte was thrown to one side as the vehicle stuttered to an ungraceful stop.

Thomas pried open the door. "Are you alright, Mrs. Wold?"

"None the worse for wear." Even as she spoke, she was consciously aware of bruises that would form on her side. Fortunately, she was wearing a woolen habit and though she snagged on one of the exposed springs, the damage could have been much worse.

"Her ladyship didn't have a spare wheel for this coach."

Of course, she didn't.

"I'll take one of the horses and go to the next town."

She pulled against gravity. "I will go with you." As she tried to exit the carriage, her ankle protested. "Ouch."

"You're injured. I'll fetch a doctor as well."

Gripping her ankle, she felt it and it didn't feel broken. "I believe I can manage. I can't stay here. It's not safe."

"I thought of that." Thomas retrieved a pistol from his waist. "Do you know how to use this?"

Unlikely as it was, she did. "Yes, my brother Nigel taught me in our youth."

"I will leave this with you, then, and travel to the next town to see if it can be repaired."

"How long will you be?"

"I'll take one of the horses and should return by nightfall."

Charlotte took the weapon and nodded. Truthfully it might be better if she remained with the carriage. There was no guarantee the wheel could be repaired or that there might be lodgings, not that she could afford them anyway.

Thomas closed the door and left.

Unfortunately, he did not return before the little remaining light was devoured by darkness.

Major Myles Ashton, desperate to escape the clutches of Devonhold, rode his horse, Ares, at a hard gallop. He was ready to return to France. He was finished meeting debutantes and their matchmaking mamas! He was tired of their disappointment in him: a second son, a soldier, and worse than all, a bastard.

Myles didn't have time for such nonsense, not with a war going on. Equality could always be found on the battlefield. Your status in life didn't matter, only your skill at weaponry, your cunning to stay alive, and your ability to defeat the enemy.

It was a moonless night, and he might have missed the dark carriage on the side of the road had it not been for the neighing of a horse as Ares passed. He reined in his horse and walked back to the carriage which was resting at an angle and missing one of its wheels.

He rapped on the black door. "Anyone in there?"

No answer. It was quiet. Had something happened to the passenger? He pulled the handle back and opened the door. "Do you require assistance?"

The click of a flintlock was a sound he recognized well.

"Go away!" a shadow answered. There wasn't enough light to see the feminine silhouette.

"Are you injured?" he asked.

"No. Go away." The air moved in front of him. She must be waving the pistol.

He backed away lest he accidentally be shot. "Do you know how to use that?"

"Yes. Now, leave. I am perfectly fine."

"Are you alone?" Who would leave a lady alone in the dark? Where was her maid, the driver, anyone?

"None of your concern," she said firmly.

"Seeing as you are stranded, ALONE, someone should be concerned."

"See here, Mister..." her voice sounded tired.

"Major," he corrected her.

"Mister Major?"

Myles heard the confusion in her voice and was tempted to laugh, but he didn't want to startle her into firing.

He chuckled softly. "Major Ashton."

"Major Ashton. I'm perfectly fine. I'm waiting for my driver to return and then I will be on my way." Her voice sounded confident and unwavering as if being stranded on the side of the road were an everyday occurrence in her world.

"Do you mind if I wait outside the carriage?"

"Why?" Her voice rose an octave. God, he wished he could see her face.

"Because it would be wrong to abandon you while your driver is absent. There could be highwaymen, you know."

A thump on the other side of the coach sounded right before the pistol fired into the carriage roof.

"Oh no! Major Ashton. Are you alive?" She clambered out of the lopsided coach, tumbled, and landed squarely on top of him. Her soft hands roamed his face and skull then fumbled along his jacket lapels before she stopped and sat up. "I see you are unharmed."

Myles could make out nothing but a shadowy figure with a crooked bonnet, still concealed by the night. "I am."

She pulled up as if he were a bed of nails. Her scrambling indicated curves, but nothing more.

"Good."

He stood, dusting himself off in the process. He looked at the carriage door.

"You are not entering the carriage," she said. He felt the flip of her clothing as she stepped in front of him.

"As you wish." Myles stepped back, allowing her to retreat into the safety of the coach.

Repeated bangs and clicks sounded as she struggled to latch the door, followed by the rumble of thunder in the distance.

Ares was getting restless, so to prevent the animal from bolting, he hitched the stallion to the carriage. It was unlikely he or the Belgian would be able to move the carriage without the wheel.

A half-hour passed before a drizzle began, which turned into a steady rain before settling into a torrential downpour.

The carriage door swung open. "You can come inside," the feminine voice capitulated.

"I'm fine." Myles pulled his coat tighter.

"You are not. Come in, you could catch a cold and die." Lightning streaked across the dark sky. He caught a glimpse of her face, delicate features with red hair and porcelain skin. Her eyes were positively luminescent as she stared at him. Though it was dark, he was certainly staring back.

"If it pleases you."

"It doesn't, however, circumstances being what they are, it seems we have no choice." Her tart voice was muffled as she retreated from the elements.

Myles stepped up into the temporary shelter.

"Stay on your side!"

"My lady, I have little choice. Gravity is working against me and you. You would be better off sitting with me than trying to cling to the opposite bench like a baby monkey."

"Why did you call me lady?" she asked.

"My apologies. It was an assumption."

"How so?"

"I recognized the crest outside your carriage, Lady Pittham."

"I'm not --"

A loud crack of thunder startled the horses, and they lurched against their harnesses to no avail, the carriage held fast by its missing wheel. All the beasts managed was to launch the lady towards him. He caught her, and the scent of lavender tickled his nose.

She gasped and struggled against his hold.

He held her firm. "Calm yourself. I will not harm you. You are safe."

A scoff was her reply.

He loosened his grip and she attempted to crawl back to her initial position.

He sighed.

The lady gave up and settled for the other side of his bench, still inclined towards him, but less so than the opposite corner.

"Why don't we try and get some sleep."

"Don't get any ideas." She warned.

He wished he could see her face. Did she look as fiery as she sounded? "Of course not, my lady."

Charlotte awoke to the sound of whistling. Thomas! She'd recognize his jaunty tune anywhere. She looked around the carriage. No sign of him. "Where is he?"

Thomas popped his head in. "Are you awake, Mrs. Wold?"

"Yes."

"My, you did have a bit of adventure." He was looking right at the hold in the ceiling.

She never should've released the hammer on the pistol. They were always more sensitive after they were cocked. "The thunder startled me." It was sort of true, there was no reason to give Thomas details.

"Sorry I didn't get back sooner, but that storm was a gully washer. I hope you didn't get too cold."

"Of course not." How could she? She'd lost the battle to stay on her side of the bench and arose in the middle of the night, with the major's arms wrapped around her. Scandalous. "Is there anyone out there with you?"

"No, mum. The wheelwright fixed it last night and I stayed in his barn. Emma Lou be happy with that, weren't you girl? Unfortunately, there were no doctor. How is your ankle?" He patted the horse and the animal whinnied as if agreeing.

She took a step out of the carriage, with no pain. "I can bear weight."

"Fine, as soon as the wheel is on, we be underway."

"Perfect." The Major had left. Lucky for her, he was a perfect gentleman. More importantly, she'd never see him again.

Chapter One

April 18, 1816 (one year later)
Devonhold Estate

Major Myles Ashton sat across from his half-brother James Fitzwilliam, Earl of Devonhold, in the study. He would rather face a firing squad than sit in this supple leather chair, forced to listen to Devonhold's latest plans for him. He drew a fortified sip of his brother's private stock of brandy. "...And of course, Lady Devonhold is honoring your homecoming with a ball."

"A ball?" Myles nearly choked on his brandy. God, he missed the war. Though he'd spent the last year behind a desk following his injury, he was not looking forward to mingling with cits who understood nothing of sacrifice.

"I am sure Amelia will keep it intimate. We only invite friends, close neighbors, and family to such gatherings."

"So, a small crush," muttered Myles with irritation.

"Do not be obtuse, Myles. It's not as if you have anywhere to go with your leg being how it is." James nodded toward the injured limb. Though his leg had fully healed, it still tended to limit physical activity. He gripped his somewhat unnecessary cane which usually served to prevent invitations to such occasions, and offered a hidden defense.

"I should probably return to London in the event Lord Palmerston requires me." The odds that the Secretary of War would need him were low, for in the past year the council of war had not convened. The Battle of Waterloo had finally seen the end of Napoleon's tyranny, and the American Colonists had ratified the Treaty of Ghent long before Myles had been shot. For this very reason, he planned to resign his commission.

"My fastest horse will carry you to London, should he need you." James knocked down his defenses.

"I have to meet with Errington." His uncle had passed away recently, naming him in his will.

"I believe he was on the guest list." Mr. Heath Errington was also his brother's solicitor. His sister-in-law, Amelia, thought nothing of mixing with the middle classes, being a former middling miss herself. Myles found her attitude refreshing.

His brother's next question caught him off guard. "What are your plans for the estate Uncle Edgar left you? There is nothing in the wilds of Scotland. Why not stay here with Amelia and me? At least you'd be with your family."

The idea of imposing on his brother did not settle well with Myles. He didn't want to admit it, but he longed to escape the proximity of London, he was done working behind a desk ensuring that the troops had supplies and that every penny was accounted for. He wasn't ready to settle down. He longed to avoid this soiree, certain Amelia would send every eligible 'miss' in attendance his way. Though he desired a family of his own eventually, there was no rush. Besides, he had no desire to engage with debutantes. They terrified him. He wanted a woman of substance, not a girl fresh from the schoolroom. His thoughts filtered back to the woman in the carriage. She'd felt so right in his arms and he had no idea who she was. A few months ago, he'd met Pelegrina Bullock, the Marchioness of Pittham, at a function in London. She was most definitely not the woman from the carriage, he'd met a year ago.

A knock on the study door interrupted his thoughts.

"Enter," James commanded.

"My lord, Lady Devonhold demanded I remind you dinner will start promptly at eight o'clock."

"So, it begins," muttered Myles. It appeared he would suffer through dinner with Lady Devonhold's debutante sisters thrown at him like cannon fire.

Nearly an hour later, after tea and biscuits, Charlotte caught a look in Amelia's eye. Her friend had a plan. Lord help her.

"That is enough, girls, let's head back to your room, and let Amelia and Charlotte talk." Arabella, Amelia's twin, possessing the same blond hair and blue eyes, rose and gestured for her younger siblings to follow her.

"But, Ara, we haven't seen Charlotte in ages," Prudence protested. She possessed the same blue eyes with spectacles and brown hair. Sadly, she was often described as plain.

"Poppycock! You've seen her every day this past year. Quit being dramatic." Amelia shooed at her sisters with her hands.

"They simply want to gossip without us," complained Maggie, who had stunning reddish-blonde hair and brown eyes, complained.

"Be that as it may, we will let them do so in peace." At the doorway, Arabella placed her hands on her hips and fixed a stern look on her face.

Once the Kendall sisters exited the drawing room, Amelia leaned toward her on the settee they shared and patted Charlotte's knee. "How are the girls treating you?"

Inwardly, she sighed with relief. She anticipated Amelia wanting some deep conversation about her future, but she had worried for naught. Her friend only wanted to check in on the status of her sisters.

"Prudence and Maggie are coming along very well. Prudence has a penchant for mathematics, and she is extremely gifted."

Amelia frowned before asking. "How is her music?"

"She struggles, but lyrical tones are not where her talent lies. Her mind is a wonder, and she should embrace her knowledge."

Amelia furrowed her brow. "To what end?"

"To better herself."

"That is all well and good, but she needs a husband," Amelia asserted.

They had this disagreement frequently during her stay. Amelia wanted the best for her sisters. Unfortunately, marriage meant security to Amelia. And why wouldn't it? Amelia had married Devonhold, a man who let his wife be her own person, who protected and loved her. Charlotte had witnessed the couple holding hands, bending their heads close in conversation, and embracing passionately several times when they thought no one noticed. Desperate to change the subject, she blurted out, "Maggie is coming along very well."

Amelia placed her hand on Charlotte's skirt. "You have done well serving as a governess to them. You are welcome to stay as long as you must. After this weekend's celebration, we will travel to London for the remainder of the Season, and you may join us there."

"Thank you, Amelia. Hopefully, London will not be necessary. I can stay here until you return," she said with demoralized firmness.

"Perhaps we might find you a husband," her friend took a bite of a biscuit.

Charlotte choked on her tea. "Why would I get married? I have responsibilities to Prudence and Maggie as their governess."

"You misunderstand me. The girls no longer require a governess. As I stated, you are welcome to stay here as long as you want, but I think a new husband is best for you."

Charlotte set the teacup in the saucer, though she longed to throw it across the room. She didn't want to get married. At eight-and-twenty, she was well on the shelf. She had some semblance of independence, and she didn't want to give that up. "I could not marry after Robert."

"Poppycock! Even I know you did not love the Reverend Wold. He was only a means to escape your parents."

She loved Amelia dearly, yet the idea of submitting to another man was vastly disagreeable. Robert had not been abusive, like her father, but he had not been affectionate, either.

Amelia continued as if Charlotte had agreed to her entire scheme. "...And truly you would not be in this position if the Reverend Wold had provided properly for you. No, the best thing to do would be to find you a husband, unless, of course, you'd like to return to the Philpotts."

Charlotte rubbed her cheek. Her father, Reverend Richard Philpott, had made his opinion about Robert very clear before she'd eloped with the man to Gretna Green. And while her mother had not been pleased either, she hadn't been quite so physical. Esther Philpott held grand plans for her daughter and Charlotte's elopement had promptly ruined years of strategy, which was unforgivable. "I do not think my returning home would be wise."

Amelia's blue eyes held a sheen of purpose. "Of course, my apologies for mentioning them. Let us set about finding you a proper husband. I believe I have the perfect candidate beneath this very roof."

"Oh?" Charlotte stiffened on the settee, her fingers gripping the cup and saucer so hard she feared the delicate porcelain might crack. She drew in a deep breath and closed her eyes.

"Yes, indeed. Devonhold's brother, well half-brother, truth be told. A bit of a scandal there, but you being such a practical woman, it would roll off your back." Amelia sailed on, and there was no stopping her friend once she set course.

"Of course." Charlotte didn't bother to argue. If Amelia didn't want independence and safety for her sisters, what chance did she have? Besides, to say no would offend Amelia, and worse, Lord Devonhold.

Amelia clapped her hands together. "Wonderful! You may meet him at dinner tonight."

"Tonight?" she gasped in a moment of panic. Meeting this favored prospect had her shaking, the saucer tinkling in her hand before she set it down. Her heart continued its rapid beat even as she gripped her gown.

"Yes, it will be a perfect opportunity for you to meet Major Ashton. He is bound to be ever so popular at the party this weekend. Truly, your timing could not be more perfect. We shall have several eligible guests for you."

Apprehension swept through Charlotte. Major Ashton! It couldn't be the same man who held her during the darkest part of the storm. She could not marry him. Then she smiled. He didn't know her identity. And once he did, it was unlikely he would want to marry her, a penniless governess.

Perhaps she could become a proper governess or if necessary, a companion instead of a wife. Yet, even to seek employment she would have to venture to London or traipse around the countryside knocking on doors. She didn't have skills in these types of things. "That sounds... nice."

"Yes!" Amelia clapped her hands. "Tonight, it will simply be Major Ashton and Viscount Kernwith, our neighbor. Fret not, Charlotte, I will provide with you the best selection of husbands."

Charlotte merely nodded. She would pretend to be interested this weekend, but she would not go to London for the Season. No. She would ask Amelia to use her connections to help install her as a governess or companion. Either was preferable to marriage.

Since Myles's arrival, he'd been interviewed by his brother, interrogated afterward by the countess, Amelia, and now his half-sister and her husband were arriving this very evening for the weekend to celebrate his brother's birthday. He did not look forward to seeing either of them.

Joan, his half-sister, the Marchioness of Worthingham, hated him. Joan's husband, Edwin Dowling, Marquess of Worthingham, was a blowhard of a man, a decade older than his wife and two decades older than Myles and James. The lord often fell asleep during dinner and if he was not snoring, his stare was haughty over the family gathered at the table because he'd been forced to marry beneath his title.

At least the likelihood of running into Joan was greatly reduced when not socializing. His room was at the far end of Devonhold, closer to the servant wing, no doubt Cobb's doing. The butler was a stickler for ranking peerage. Cobb would've had the housekeeper install Amelia's sisters near the servants if it did not reveal the butler's disdain. A smile lit his face as he imagined Lord and Lady Worthingham having to room so close to the young ladies, Prudence and Magdalene. No doubt the Kendall girls would keep his harpy of a sister up all night with their giggling.

Myles pulled his uncle's worn timepiece from his pocket. The gold plain-faced watch was one of the many unusual items given to him by Edgar. Myles held fond memories of the man. His uncle was more affectionate toward him in his last thirty years of life than his father had ever been. The Honorable Edgar Fitzwilliam had purchased his commission and before his military career, he had sent many gifts over the years, like the pocket watch.

As Myles changed into his evening clothes, he noted with a sense of sadness Uncle Edgar had given him essentially the life he now lived. A shame the man died. He would never be able to thank him.

Myles was relieved the housekeeper hadn't assigned many servants to this end of the wing. Nonetheless, the maids were irritatingly attentive. No fewer than three had asked if he'd like a bath drawn. The last one had entered with water, claiming to have the wrong room. He shook his head at the nonsense of females.

Myles finished dressing for dinner and glanced into the looking glass to make sure his cravat wasn't askew before exiting his room. He wore his red uniform. Soon enough he would be a cit and would make the necessary wardrobe accommodations. As he closed the door, he heard a simultaneous click behind him. Years of war and instinct forced him to pivot and face this new challenge. His leg objected and he released a moan.

"Are you all right?"

Standing before him was the woman who had been ever-present in his mind this past year. If possible, she was perhaps more lovely. He scanned her and couldn't distinguish the curves he recalled the night he held her. She wore a drab gown. Was she a servant in his brother's house? And how had she arrived here?

"Major Ashton?" she tested her voice. She gripped the door handle behind her. Her entire stance indicated she was ready to flee.

Curiosity overrode his manners. "Who are you?"

She released the handle and fisted her hands at her sides before taking a step toward him. "I am Charlotte Wold. Widow of the late Reverend Wold."

Her light red hair was pulled back from her face and her wide gray eyes were a smokescreen. "Oh, I remember you, Mrs. Wold. A man doesn't forget a woman he held in his arms."

Her lips trembled and she looked right then left before spinning around to face her door but didn't open it. Her breath was the only audible sound.

"Damnation," he muttered. He was an absolute bastard.

She turned her head toward him but kept her hand on the knob.

Myles ran a hand through his hair. "My apologies. I didn't mean to malign your reputation; it was my poor attempt at humor."

Her rose lips drew up like a bow in a half-smile revealing enchanting dimples. "I accept your poor attempt at an apology. I shall, however, remain skeptical of your humor."

"Understandable. May I escort you to dinner?" Myles closed the distance between them and offered his arm. Though etiquette dictated he call her Mrs. Wold, he longed to call her Charlotte. A lovely name.

"No, thank you." Her chin held high, she pushed past him, descended the stairs, and navigated silently to the dining room.

He followed her, watching the sway of dark fabric wave side to side like a war banner.

When they arrived at the dining room, there were two remaining seats next to Arabella and one nestled between Prudence and Magdalene. He was certain this was Amelia's doing.

Pierce Ellis, Viscount of Kernwith, cleared his throat behind them.

Arabella waved and patted the seat next to her. Charlotte advanced to take the chair. Not about to concede, Myles followed the widow in and sighed, "Poor Kernwith."

Charlotte gave him a sidelong glance and raised her delicate eyebrows. He swore he glimpsed a ghost of a smirk.

Myles couldn't help but grant her a winsome smile. Who was she, and why was she here? The mystery of Charlotte Wold would prove an adequate distraction. Dinner with family would be as easy as commanding loyal soldiers.

Chapter Two

As the servants were clearing the soup bowls, Myles changed his mind, nothing with his family was simple. He was certain death—very possibly murder—would occur before he left this room. He was relieved he would not be involved, but he made no guarantees about the women at the table.

"I am afraid Amelia is correct, Mrs. Wold. You need to find a husband," his half-sister, the marchioness, was dictating. "I doubt you'll be able to reach as far above your station as Lady Devonhold, but certainly someone will be found."

"Not every woman desires a husband," Arabella wrinkled her nose.

"Nor every man a wife," Viscount Kernwith responded.

"There is a truer statement if ever spoken," the Marquess of Worthingham commented to the table at large.

"Such a statement could not have been true for you, Worthingham." Joan clutched at the violet material above her cold heart as if her husband grievously wounded her.

"No, my lady, you well and truly earned your prize." Lord Worthingham nodded toward his wife.

"It would seem I was not the *only* one to marry above my station," Amelia commented as the servers brought in a venison roast with root vegetables.

Myles smiled at his plate, silently cheering his brother's wife on.

"I am curious what Charlotte thinks," Prudence asked.

He also wanted to know the widow's views.

"I have been married and my husband has since passed," she commented.

"I understood the Reverend Wold was killed over a year ago, wasn't it?" Lady Worthingham asked.

"Yes," Charlotte responded to her venison.

"You can't still be grieving. Especially given where and how he died." Lady Worthingham gave a most unladylike snort before continuing. "You do not have time to dawdle with your emotions."

Charlotte stiffened and met the lady's stare. "I am not."

"Well, then please share your thoughts," Lady Worthingham insisted.

Though Myles believed his sister's behavior was at the height of rudeness, he wanted to hear Charlotte's response. Was she made of sterner stuff?

Charlotte looked at the table. Everyone waited for her to respond. What to say? Her husband had found her so repulsive he fled to his mistress, Lisette, at every chance and that was where he met his demise. Robert had not bedded her in the years before his death. Something must be wrong with her. Did they all see it? Her gaze rested on the man seated next to her.

She was finally getting a chance to see Major Myles Ashton after their last encounter. His green eyes regarded her with curiosity, his hardened features were smooth, and his head tilted in question. The uniform he wore gave him a dashing look, with a bit of danger. The cane at his side was also new, but perhaps the injury was shortly after they had met.

"I believe a woman is fortunate if she can marry for love." Charlotte glanced toward Amelia and then to her husband, James.

"Nonsense. A woman cannot have such luxury," the marquess bellowed from his end of the table.

"Spoken like a man who only has sons and no daughters to contend with," Lord Devonhold argued.

"What are you going on about?" Lord Worthingham bristled. "You have no offspring. Heirs, bastards, or otherwise."

Major Ashton gripped his silverware so hard his knuckles turned white. He was dangerous.

"True, but I have three new sisters to see settled, and I am sure my wife would want their feelings considered." Lord Devonhold smiled fondly at each of the Kendalls.

Charlotte pursed her lips to keep from speaking. She didn't want to disrespect her hosts. Maybe Amelia believed everyone could find love. Blessed to be part of Amelia's family and their camaraderie she basked in their warmth, which she desperately needed to banish her cynicism. She would appreciate the time spent with them, however brief.

Much to her relief, the remainder of dinner continued without a further discussion of her marital prospects. Following dessert, the ladies withdrew to the drawing room while the unmarried Kendalls were ushered to bed by Arabella. Lord Devonhold opted to forego the separation of the sexes, and the gentlemen joined the ladies for coffee and tea. However, they did not sit as much as they loitered with their drinks inside the door.

Charlotte suspected this ruffled Lord and Lady Worthingham's proper feathers, especially after the marchioness' inappropriate broach on the subject of inheritance. "So, Uncle Edgar has left you that abhorrent hunting lodge he purchased along with the ruins of Mosswin Castle?"

Major Ashton winced at his half-sister's question, but answered, "It would appear so."

"You men and your hunting! You are fortunate you meant so much to him. He always did dote on you. It is just like the old coot to leave you a dingy old castle." Lady Worthingham took a hearty sip of tea.

Major Ashton went visibly rigid. "I am waiting on Errington to send along the details."

"There would be a good candidate for Mrs. Wold." Lady Worthingham looked to Charlotte, "Mr. Errington is both Ashton's and James' man of business."

But not Lord and Lady Worthingham's, so not too far above Charlotte. Would this be the topic of conversation at every event she attended? Unless she voiced her opinion on marriage and husbands, these people were determined to find her an eligible bachelor.

Gathering her courage, Charlotte said, "I am not certain if Mr. Errington is for me."

"He is a very nice man," Amelia assured her.

"I am sure he is." Charlotte looked to Major Ashton and Viscount Kernwith. She chose her next words carefully so as not to offend. "I may not be marriage material any longer."

"Poppycock," Amelia waved. "You are not so far on the shelf."

Charlotte agreed but didn't say so.

Major Ashton inspected her, but his eyes were flat and unreadable. She could only imagine what he must think given their previous meeting in Lady Pittham's carriage.

"Mrs. Wold does have a point. Most men want a young wife, and she *was* married to Reverend Wold for nearly ten years with no children. Perhaps she is barren."

"Lady Worthingham!" The marquess roared from the other side of the room, nearly choking on his port.

His wife was quick to respond. "I am sorry. If my brother let you men have your port in the dining room, perhaps your masculine ears would be spared the ins and outs of the Marriage Mart. Be happy I gave you sons, thus you won't have to be subjected to what is required when launching a debutante, let alone a widow."

Charlotte wanted to sink into the floral fabric of the chair.

Lord Worthingham frowned. "Such a falsehood, my dear. As if your marriage machinations would be limited when David and Daniel search for brides."

"Such a search is many years away, my lord," she assured him.

The marquess shook his head at his wife.

"Be that as it may, I do like Mr. Errington as a prospect for Charlotte." Amelia smiled at her friend.

"Mr. Errington may have an opinion or two," Viscount Kernwith remarked.

"At this time, Mr. Errington is irrelevant. We are discussing Charlotte." Amelia said.

Of course, they were. She was starting to believe there was no hope for her to escape the marriage trap her friend had set.

Lady Worthington scowled as she looked past the men. "Is Mr. Errington arriving at Devonhold regarding your estate, then, Ashton?"

Major Ashton nodded. "I understand he is invited."

"Well, when he arrives, we will extend his stay. Do you not agree, James?" Amelia asked.

"Of course, my dear." Lord Devonhold beamed at his wife.

Charlotte sipped her tea. She had tried and yet failed to accurately express her opinions. She stole a glance at Major Ashton.

He offered a small smile, yet his gaze traveled the length of her as if he, too, found her deficient. Heat rose in her cheeks, and she sat taller before she shot him a withering look.

Major Ashton nodded as if accepting her challenge.

Chapter Three

Mr. Heath Errington arrived the following morning and was, as predicted, invited to stay the remainder of the weekend.

He lounged in a leather chair, mesmerized by the amber liquid in his glass. "And you're certain your sister-in-law is planning to make a match for me?" Errington leaned forward in his chair.

"I believe she plans to make a match for every eligible bachelor beneath her roof before the sun rises Monday morning." Myles was duty-bound to warn Errington of Lady Amelia's plans. Cautioning the man was the least he could do; after all, they'd grown up together. Errington's father had been the late earl's solicitor, and Myles and Errington were tutored separately from James and Joan. Hell, Myles couldn't very well let his old friend be caught in the matrimonial noose.

"So how many bucks are there, then?" Errington nodded.

"The two of us and the newly titled neighbor, Viscount Kernwith," Myles confessed.

"Pierce Ellis?" Errington asked.

Myles shook his head at fate's humor. "The very same. Who would've guessed a groundskeeper's son would become a lord of the realm?"

"And eligible ladies?" Errington returned the conversation to Lady Amelia's well-laid plans. He always was more curious than cautious. The man was a genius with numbers yet couldn't see the problem in front of his nose. A debutante was to be avoided at all costs. Although given Errington's lack of title, he was unlikely to be targeted by marriage-minded misses and their scheming mamas.

"Lady Amelia's three sisters and the widow Wold."

"You would count the widow?" Errington looked puzzled.

"I would. You should've seen her, Errington. It was harrowing to watch Joan dig into her like a cat tortures a mouse." Despite his misgivings, Myles sensed a bit of kinship with Charlotte. She was the only woman who interested him. She wasn't immature like Magdalene and Prudence, and Arabella's resemblance to Amelia discomfited him. The pull toward Charlotte was present ever since the night he'd first met her. Charlotte Wold possessed hidden steel.

"Shall I consider her?"

"No, you shall not." Myles didn't know why he was so possessive of the widow. Perhaps because she was the only woman in his memory since that fateful, yet brief, meeting. He'd even considered asking Lady Pittham about the woman in the carriage but thought better of it. He hadn't wanted to ruin a woman's reputation. To think this whole time she had been at his brother's country estate as a governess. Was Charlotte still in mourning given her resistance to Amelia's matchmaking? Her behavior was odd to him, but he didn't have much experience with women. Perhaps, as his sister suggested, she was barren. That would be a disappointment to any man who threw in for her, needing an heir. Since he had no intention of doing such a thing, it didn't bother him a whit.

"Indeed." Errington raised a dark eyebrow at him.

"Keep your opinions to yourself," Myles warned him. He leaned back, taking a sip of his brother's private stock of Scotch Whisky, and promptly changed the subject. "Tell me about my estate."

Errington removed papers from his satchel, placing them on the mahogany desk in front of Myles. "I looked over the entailment with your uncle's solicitor, and everything appears to be in order. According to the documentation, you are the Honorable Edgar Fitzwilliam's sole heir."

"How can that be?"

"I asked that very question and was not told the reason by the late lord's solicitor, who said it would be clarified when you arrive at Mosswin Castle."

Myles tapped the tumbler against his lips, considering this.

Errington shook his head. "I found it peculiar as well, but I didn't press the man on the matter."

Myles set his glass on the desk. His fingers touched parchment, and he pulled the document toward him. "What can you tell me about the property?"

Errington set his scotch next to Myles' glass. "I have not seen it myself, but it sounds as if the castle may require repairs. However, the cottage seems to be in order. Perhaps the reason you were not notified is due to... how shall I explain this?"

"Spit it out, man!"

Errington stood. "As I understand it, there are residents."

"Residents?" He gripped his cane tight.

"Yes, and it is a sticky wicket. It seems your uncle's mistress and her daughter reside on the property." Errington paced the floor.

Myles barked with laughter. "The devil, you say?"

Errington rubbed his temples. "And as part of the entailment, you will need to take the girl as your ward."

"And the mistress?"

"She has agreed to leave if you wish her to do so, upon your possession of Mosswin," Errington replied.

"Edgar never did follow convention. It does not matter if my cousin and her mother stay." Myles reached for his glass and drank, and let the scotch warm him. He envied his uncle. The man had lived a life doing as he pleased and unanswerable to anyone. Though it was dastardly, Myles mourned the loss of the war. He had no idea what to do with life among the cits. But if he was to be one, then he'd rather do it in Scotland, away from the *ton* and their judgment.

Charlotte had been perched so long upon the dressmaker's box that she was certain her feet had planted roots. She stood ramrod straight as Madame Bristol clucked about the dark blue fabric, placing a pin here and a pin there. The gown being altered was almost black until light illuminated the fabric and revealed hints of blue.

"You are fortunate Amelia already had the modiste prepare dresses for her sisters," Lady Worthingham droned on.

"We are most fortunate Madame Bristol created this lovely dress requiring but a few adjustments," Amelia commented.

Charlotte frowned at her friend. She knew very well this dress was intended for Amelia's wardrobe, not for the dance this evening. "Thank you."

"Poppycock, it is nothing, my dear. Granting you a small wardrobe is the least I can do."

"Especially when my brother is footing the bill." Lady Worthingham assessed Charlotte as if deciding whether Lord Devonhold's coin was worth the effort.

"You'll see, Lady Worthingham, the wardrobe will assist in catching a husband," Amelia assured the matron.

Not this subject again.

"We'll see." Lady Worthingham countered.

"Perhaps I should invest in a riding habit, rather than a gown since we are hunting," Charlotte said dryly.

"I think I have a lovely habit that would require minimal alterations," Madame Bristol chimed in with her grating accent.

Amelia smiled and shook her head. "Perhaps the next time, Madame."

"You are not far off, Mrs. Wold," Lady Worthingham frowned as she examined the modiste's samples. "So have any of the men caught your eye? Mr. Errington arrived this morning, and I glimpsed him as he entered James's study. He is not a bad-looking gent."

Charlotte didn't disagree. Mr. Heath Errington was quite handsome with his blue eyes and black hair even if perhaps he was a bit younger. Major Ashton was much more appealing. His rich brown hair lessened the severity of his deep green eyes, a hawkish nose, and the stubborn set of his chin.

"Charlotte?" Amelia waved her hand in front of her face.

She was caught off-guard by Amelia's vibrant voice. "Yes?"

"Lady Worthingham asked you a question."

"Perchance she is daydreaming about her prospects now?" Lady Worthingham gave her a knowing grin.

The heat of a flush crept along her exposed neckline.

"I think you may be correct, Joan," Amelia agreed and winked at Charlotte.

"Megnofick!" Madame Bristol proclaimed in her horrible faux-French, stepping away and admiring her handiwork. "I took the dress out in the bustline, but I think *eet* will serve you well, Mrs. Wold."

Charlotte turned to look in the full-length-looking glass. The subtle color changes created a magical illusion of moving shadows. The dark material subdued her freckled skin while her gray eyes shimmered with the fabric.

"I must admit Amelia, you do far better with so little to work with. I had not imagined you capable," Lady Worthington complimented.

"Thank you, Joan. I can't claim all the credit. Madame Bristol is an artist, and it helps to have sisters ready to launch in the Marriage Mart. Shall we head to the parlor for tea?" Amelia asked.

Lady Worthington quickened her pace to the door. "Do you know what pastries Chef Andre has prepared?"

Amelia followed. "I believe some variations of spice cakes. Are you coming, Charlotte?"

"I am afraid not. I have developed a bit of a megrim." She placed her thumb and forefingers on her brow and winced her eyes. She wasn't ready to discuss her marriage prospects. A plan to escape the matchmaking was necessary. But what? She needed to find a solution to homelessness before she was dragged to London's Marriage Mart.

Amelia spoke as she closed the door. "I'll have a tray sent up. Take a rest. You'll need your strength for dancing tonight."

Charlotte enjoyed her tea and spice cake in the privacy of her room. The peace allowed her to nap and relax, not because she intended to dance into the wee hours of the night, but because she was timeworn from the day's events. Amelia meant well, but she had no intention of being inspected at the dance like a prize pony. Unfortunately, a husband usually was the answer to most lady's problems. In her opinion, matrimony was not a mistake to be made twice. Better to remain a widow.

The midnight blue dress was sent to her room after alterations were completed, and one of the maids helped her don the garment with expediency. She sat at her dressing table, waiting for Monique to come and do her hair.

A knock came at the door.

Charlotte smiled, ready to begin. "Come in."

A young maid with brown hair peeking beneath the lace of her mob cap poked her head in. "Mrs. Wold?"

"Yes."

The maid gave an almost hesitant nod. "My name is Lizzy. I've been assigned to do your hair. Monique is busy with the other ladies."

"I am sure you'll do perfectly fine." Charlotte smiled at Lizzy, who wouldn't meet her gaze.

Lizzy shuffled in with a basket on her arm. It was full of brushes, combs, pins, and a small assortment of ribbons. She set it on the vanity. "You'll be my first."

Charlotte escaped into thoughts and anxiety settled in. She'd planned to feign illness to be released from the evening's obligations but now she wasn't so sure. Once Lizzy styled her hair, she would reassess her plan.

Lizzy began brushing. "You have lovely hair, Mum."

"Thank you." The tug on her hair reminded Charlotte of her youth and her mother preparing her for parties to find a rich suitor. She frowned as she recalled her wishes went unheard. Charlotte hadn't chosen well though when she'd married Robert Wold. How wrong she had been. He was never home and was always with his mistress. Why had he bothered to marry her? Was it for respectability or something else? It certainly hadn't been for her.

"Do you have a style preference?" Lizzy's question caught her off guard.

Charlotte hadn't expected a choice in the matter. Much like her childhood, she assumed it would be dictated by either Amelia or perhaps even Lady Worthington. "Honestly, I hadn't considered it."

Lizzy tilted her head. "If I may recommend a style?"

"You may." What did it matter? It wasn't as if anyone would see it while she stayed locked in her room.

"Your hair is such a lovely color, I will pull it loosely back into a chignon and run this matching ribbon through it," Lizzy said.

Charlotte found the maid's tone comforting. "Your suggestion sounds perfect."

Lizzy drew long brush strokes through her hair. She pulled the tresses back and away from her face before finally winding it into the chignon. The maid then wound the ribbon over and under her hair until the fabric was weaved through as if it had always been present.

"Lizzy, this is..." Charlotte didn't know what to say as she angled the handheld mirror toward the larger-looking glass. "Thank you."

"You're welcome, mum. This works better with your wavy hair. You have those natural wisps which come forward and frame your face."

After Lizzy left, Charlotte couldn't help but stare at the beauty in the mirror. Gone was the drab widow of the late Reverend Wold. She had been transformed into an unrecognizable woman who could be courted and possibly even rival the current flock of debutantes.

Charlotte wanted to go to the dance, but all the earlier talk of marriage dampened her enthusiasm. Perhaps she could wait a bit until the excitement of the evening settled. She smiled at the idea. She would slip downstairs to the garden and avoid the crush of eligible roosters chasing her about the ballroom as if she were a hen in the barnyard.

Charlotte sat for nearly an hour before she exited her room. She found the hallway refreshingly empty. She turned left and tiptoed. Navigation was easy enough, for her room was practically stationed at the top of the back steps. As expected, the house was vacant with all servants working below. Nevertheless, she descended as quietly as possible. There was no need to draw unnecessary attention.

Once at the bottom landing, Charlotte exited through the back of the house stepping softly toward the garden. She followed the cobbled walk bordering the house before rounding the path toward where the balcony glowed with lantern light casting away the shadows. As she hoped, the party was still contained indoors. She cautiously approached the balcony steps, closely watching for emerging guests. As the foliage thinned, she peered across and through the line of French doors. Many attendees were still dancing, and all eyes were on the ballroom floor.

Charlotte sighed a breath she didn't know she was holding. Why was she worried? After all, she was a widow, not some young debutante whose reputation required protection. She glided up the steps. Her interest in the ball increased with each footfall. Once she reached the top, she sought a bench off to the side where she could watch the guests behind glass and calm her racing heart.

"I was wondering when you would arrive," Major Myles Ashton's deep and sensual voice broke through the darkness.

Charlotte missed the bench and landed hard in a topiary.

Chapter Four

Myles almost failed to notice Charlotte as she slipped silently through the garden. Her dress was the color of midnight, making it nearly impossible to see her. However, there was no mistaking the way her skin glowed in the moonlight, or the way lamplight flickered over her vibrant red hair. She moved tentatively forward, peering around the corner.

Once he'd made his presence known and scared her off-balance into the shrubbery, Myles was obligated to step out of the shadows to offer his assistance. He was too pleased with her presence to regret startling her.

She crossed her arms, staring daggers at him. "Where did you come from?"

He smiled at her, his arm still outstretched. "Much like you, I was hiding in the shadows. I wish I'd considered an entrance via the garden."

She finally accepted his help, and he pulled her from the now-decapitated swan she'd landed in. Her gloves prevented a more intimate touch. Such was his penance for scaring her. "You saw me?" A blush crept along her skin before she shook his hold until she was free.

He longed to discover if her blushed flesh would be hot beneath his touch. She smoothed her skirts of imaginary dirt and leaves. "You are not as invisible as you might wish. At least not to me." All his senses had honed in on her. He still couldn't explain the sensation that drew his eye toward her approach.

"You are not invisible at all." She nodded at his uniform.

Myles snorted before giving her an elegant bow. "True, however, being seen is the point of these events."

Her face turned sour. "No, the point is to catch a husband."

"You do not wish for a husband?" he asked, fascinated. She must be one of the few females here who didn't have matrimony on her mind. Of course, she was a widow. He furrowed his brow at the reminder of her late husband. He dearly hoped she wasn't still pining for the man.

"I've already had one. Why would I want another?" She edged closer to the bench overlooking the walkways before seating herself.

"I hear they can be beneficial." He couldn't fathom what possessed him to encourage such talk. His hands clenched at his sides, imagining Charlotte in another man's arms.

"Then *you* go find one," she retorted.

Myles couldn't stop the laughter that burst forth. He found her candor refreshing. "I can't. Don't you know? I must find a wife to beget my heir."

She glanced into the ballroom. "It would appear you have quite the selection."

"All of them aged sixteen to nineteen." He shuddered.

She raised her chin. "I would assume young debutantes are ideal to supply heirs."

He shook his head. "Why would I want to marry a chit nearly half my age?"

She gave him a dumbfounded look. "Isn't youth what every gentleman seeks in a bride?"

"Perhaps like yourself, I am not ready to be leg-shackled, just yet."

"I can see, with your cane, how leg shackling would impede you." She quickly covered her lips.

He smiled, unoffended by her humor. "So, you've got a bit of bite."

Her chin dipped down, but not before he glimpsed her flushed cheeks. "I am sorry. My comment was horribly rude. I do not know what came over me. I must beg your forgiveness."

Inspiration struck him. "I'll grant my forgiveness for a favor."

"What favor?" Her pink lips pressed into a firm line.

He offered his hand. "Would you allow me to escort you into the dance?"

"That would be unwise. People will talk." She bit her lower lip and her gray eyes cast downward.

He withdrew his hand, curious how she would sidestep him. "What will they say?"

"They will think we have formed an attachment." Her voice was a hushed whisper, and yet it sounded like a warning bell to his ears. *What was she afraid of?*

"And if they do?" He raised an eyebrow. "What do you care? What do I?"

"It may complicate your efforts to find a bride to beget your heir."

"Or perhaps, they will want what you already have, making me all the more desirable."

"Major, if anything, they would wonder why you are with me. Amelia and your sister will consider me even more of a charity case."

"Oh?"

"Amelia no longer requires my services."

"As a governess?" He had learned her place within the household at dinner.

"Yes."

"So, with your position ending, what will you do?"

"I'm not certain. But I will not take on the role of wife, I can assure you."

"Why don't you let me escort you in, and let people think what they may."

"I barely know you. You do not want to marry, and I do not want--" The moment she grasped his plan, an irresistible smile spread across her face, revealing lovely dimples. "We won't be forced to participate in these ridiculous, however well-intentioned, rituals."

Charlotte was a clever woman. "You are quick of wit."

She rose in one fluid motion. "Major Ashton, you are a true strategist! You must be sorely missed by your men in the field."

"Thank you, Mrs. Wold. For our ruse to work, I permit you to call me Myles or Ashton if you prefer." He was rather proud of himself. Though she didn't know it, at another time he may have courted her. The easiest way to forego the matchmaking was for everyone to believe their charade.

"And you may call me Charlotte, Ashton."

He offered his arm. "Well, Charlotte, will you do me the honor?"

"I believe I will." She linked her arm with his, and they walked into the ballroom together.

Charlotte stiffened once they crossed the threshold. Silence fell over the room as they entered between sets. All eyes turned toward them: young debutantes, perhaps eyeing the prize of Major Ashton for themselves, older matrons tisking at the image of long-in-the-tooth Charlotte catching a man beyond her class; and the men... who knew what they must think of the widow Wold on the arm of Major Ashton, the brother of an earl! She didn't want Myles, no matter how attractive he was. But his tactic would buy her time as she formulated a better plan, and it would prevent her from offending Amelia.

After the open-mouthed stares came to a halt, the whispers began. Giggles behind fans. Gentlemen nodded toward Myles. She liked the name, Myles, however, calling him Ashton would relate their informality without undue intimacy. His plan to associate with one another would serve until she resolved her situation.

He gave her arm a light press with his fingers, drawing her eyes to his face. "Shall I escort you to Lady Devonhold?"

"Yes, I would like to speak with her, now that tongues are wagging."

"This will work, Charlotte, I promise," he reassured her.

She nodded, mutely. She believed him. She sensed Major Ashton was an honest man. Perhaps it was his green eyes which were both inquisitive and playful. He was certainly an agreeable and well-bred gentleman. A pang of regret surfaced. A gentleman would never belong to her, and why would she want one? Charlotte needed to find a solution that didn't involve a man, even one as desirable as Ashton. No, she needed to rescue herself from Amelia and all the other well-intentioned matrons.

They arrived at Amelia's side. "Here we are, my dear. I leave you in capable hands." Ashton raised her gloved hand to his lips.

A gasp arose from the ladies.

He smiled and winked at her before departing.

"I see Major Ashton has taken a fancy to you," Amelia drawled.

"Yes. I rather like him as well," Charlotte replied, honestly.

Lady Worthington snapped her fan shut. "How did this come about?"

"We found we had much in common." Such as avoiding matrimony.

"Oh, are you a bastard as well?" Lady Worthington sneered.

Amelia's eyebrows climbed in a frigid arch. "Joan!"

Lady Worthington shrugged. "What? She's going to discover his sin sooner or later. If Mrs. Wold is serious about my half-brother, she should know the truth." She sipped her punch.

"His birth is something Major Ashton should share with her, not the gossip mill," Amelia stated.

"It's not gossip. He *is* a bastard. Born only ten days after James, Devonhold's rightful heir." Lady Worthington thrust her chin up.

Charlotte was too startled to respond. Breeding did not always include proper manners. She had wondered why the last name was Ashton and not Fitzwilliam, but she didn't dwell on it. Regardless of his birth, she had no intention of marrying him or any other man. The more time she spent with the upper classes, the more she wanted the peace of country life. Damn Robert, for getting shot.

"Do not worry, Charlotte. Major Ashton is not as bad as Lady Worthington claims." Amelia patted her arm.

"I am sure not." During her short stay, she deduced the aged matron had a flair for the dramatic.

"Did you not even consider my brother's solicitor, Mr. Errington?" Lady Worthington asked.

"Ashton made an offer I could not in good faith refuse." Charlotte tamped down the guilt at her version of the truth.

"Did he?" Amelia asked, tilting her head to the side.

Had she revealed too much? Amelia and Lady Worthington probably knew better than anyone whether Myles would offer for her, let alone any eligible miss. "Well, not a proposal of marriage, but we've agreed to get to know one another based on our common interests."

"And what would those be?" Lady Worthington asked.

What indeed? "Literary pursuits," she blurted.

"Myles was always a connoisseur of literature," Amelia confirmed.

"I suppose there are few cultural pursuits when one is at war," Lady Worthington agreed.

Charlotte's heart settled back to a normal pace as the ladies moved on from Myles, in particular, to speak of men in general.

"Viscount Kernwith seems taken with Arabella," Lady Worthington pointed out.

"Indeed, but she is *not* so taken with him," said Amelia.

Charlotte watched the young couple from across the room, and the expression on Arabella's face indicated she was far from impressed. "It seems as if Magdalene and Prudence are sharing an admirer."

"Mr. Heath Errington," Lady Worthington's voice lowered to a near whisper.

"He is very attractive, but he looks younger." The young man between them held an air of mystery with his swarthy skin, dark hair, and blue eyes. However, she did not feel the same pull as she did with Ashton.

"Mrs. Wold, you are wise. I believe he is only five and twenty. I can attest marrying an older man is far better than a younger one who is perhaps not ready for matrimony." Lady Worthington sailed on. "Mr. Errington is likely flirting shamelessly with those girls."

"Do you think he is, Joan?"

"Yes. You should put an end to it."

Amelia's eyebrows drew together in a pained expression. "I could, but you know siblings. They never listen to you, even though you have their best interests at heart."

Lady Worthington bobbed her head in commiseration. "I am well aware. My condolences."

"Joan, I hate to impose." Amelia shook her head. "No, I dare not ask."

"Would you like me to speak with them?" Lady Worthington asked, clearly eager to impart her wisdom to a younger generation.

Amelia tilted her head. "If you would not mind terribly. I feel your standing would bear more weight than my own."

"Of course. As we are family, I would be happy to assist in this matter." Lady Worthington launched forward to do her familial duty.

"You goaded her on purpose," Charlotte said once the matron had engaged the Kendall sisters in conversation.

"It was the only way to get rid of the old harridan." Amelia rested her hands on Charlotte's arm. "Now, tell me, what is going on with Myles?"

"It is as I said, we have common literary pursuits."

Amelia wrinkled her brow. "Truly? Major Ashton does not strike me as a bibliophile."

"You do not know," she protested.

"You are correct. I have no idea if the man likes Chaucer, Shakespeare, or Lord Byron." Amelia's gaze penetrated her calm. "And neither do you, Charlotte Wold."

She lifted her chin and met Amelia's gaze. "Does it matter? You were recommending Ashton earlier."

"I did, didn't I?" Her expression stilled.

"Yes, so what is at issue now?" Charlotte was curious, seeing this change in her friend.

"Well, he is a soldier, and I am worried his intentions toward you may not be entirely honorable."

"How a man acts is far more important than what he may intend." Charlotte's late husband had been considered honorable, and yet his actions belied the truth. Perhaps when they were first married, Robert had the best intentions. He had hoped his marriage to her would benefit him in the *ton*. When his plans didn't come to fruition, he blamed her. His bad luck and failure were laid at her feet.

"As long as you are certain."

Charlotte shivered. "I am." She would *certainly never* marry again.

Chapter Five

James swung the door open so hard it slammed against the wall. "What are your intentions toward the widow?"

Myles choked on his port. He frowned. Sometimes his brother didn't know when to stay silent. "None of your business."

"Whatever you do, do not bed her." James scowled at him. "I have to live with the consequences of your actions."

"I have honorable intentions." Myles dared his brother to suggest otherwise.

"Honor seems highly unlikely," James scoffed.

"You believe I would bed Charlotte without accepting the consequences?" He didn't mind the idea of bedding her, but he'd never say such a thing. Myles didn't care for others to think of her as a loose woman.

"*Charlotte*, is it?" James smirked. "If you do indeed bed her, it is possible there would be no consequences. She was married for seven years without any offspring to show."

The mention of her husband gave him pause to indulge his curiosity. "You are assuming *she* is the reason no children came from her union. It is simply as likely the devout Reverend Wold may have been at fault. Wasn't he significantly older?"

"No. I believe they were of the same age. I met the man at our wedding and did not care for him. He was a bit of a toad," James answered.

"Do you believe it was a love match?" A happy union would explain why Charlotte was perhaps not eager to leap once again into matrimony. He didn't know why but Myles would be rather disappointed if she still loved her husband.

"Who can say? Besides, I am more concerned you'll leave a broken heart in your wake. Amelia would likely bar me from consequences for a fortnight," James said with a bit of a chuckle.

Myles smiled. "It would serve you right for meddling in my affairs."

Errington approached them. "Who is having an affair?"

"No one," both men answered.

"Did my sister chase you away from your quarry?" James looked beyond Errington to where the younger Kendall sisters stood presently guarded by Joan.

"She *did* scare me. However, being among bachelors suits me fine. Your new family members are a bit too young and too frivolous. I see you've laid claim to the Widow Wold. Well done, Ashton." Errington slapped him on the back.

"I haven't laid anything," Myles said, irritated. He wished they would leave well enough alone. His personal life was his own. Did every person in attendance this weekend need to involve themselves in his bachelorhood?

"He's a bit touchy about the subject of the widow," James confided.

"Ah," replied Errington with a double raise of the eyebrows. "It is probably just as well since she seems to be dancing presently with the fresh and honorable Lord Kernwith."

The strains of a popular waltz filled the room, but Charlotte's dance partner seemed entirely unaware of its meter.

"I'm not stepping on your toes, am I?" Viscount Kernwith asked.

"You are doing fine." Charlotte winced. The truth was, he was an abysmal dancer.

"Kind of you to say so. However, I am aware I have two left feet." He nearly nicked her small toe.

"Then why did you ask me to dance?" Charlotte couldn't hide the irritation in her voice. She should not have agreed, but she was still reeling from Ashton's brilliant tactic.

"Truthfully?"

"Please." She preferred honesty. Lord knew she hadn't had much in her short life.

He leaned forward and lowered his voice. "I needed a distraction from Miss Kendall."

"Which one?"

"Arabella." He stared at the 'Miss' in question, which caused him to misstep once again in a dance he hadn't mastered and had no business leading her in.

She side-stepped his foot, again. "May I ask what exactly about her upsets you?"

"She doesn't like me."

"Oh? Do you know why?" Perhaps he'd crushed Arabella's toes in a set.

He wiped all semblance of feeling from his face. "I have no idea, but she is a termagant of the highest order."

"I see." Although she didn't. Lord Kernwith lacked skill. So why ask her to dance? Charlotte's feet were forced to suffer the young lord's inexperience.

They finished their set, none too soon for Charlotte. She turned and caught Ashton frowning at them from his corner of the dance floor. Heat crept along her skin. "My lord, would you be so kind as to escort me to Major Ashton?"

"He is standing next to Miss Arabella." The panic in his voice was palpable.

"I doubt she will cause a scene in front of the major," Charlotte assured him.

"We could dance another set," he suggested.

Lord, her toes wouldn't survive, nor her reputation. "I am afraid dancing anymore would be highly inappropriate." She used her sternest tone, the very same voice she used when Prue and Maggie would get out of hand.

Viscount Kernwith acknowledged this and trudged in the direction of Ashton and Arabella, albeit dragging their feet. At least her own were finally safe.

Ashton watched them as they approached.

Charlotte gave him her best smile, and he returned a frown. She couldn't resist teasing him. "You know, Major, if you continue frowning your face will freeze."

Ashton shook his head. "My dear, on the off chance it is true, I am willing to take the risk."

"Perhaps Major Ashton's expression is an indicator he is more serious than those of the peerage." Arabella leveled her gaze on Viscount Kernwith.

Charlotte agreed with the viscount. Miss Kendall did *not* like him.

"Major Ashton, would you mind escorting me to the punch bowl?"

"Certainly, Mrs. Wold." He offered his arm.

Lord Kernwith refused to release her. "I can escort you."

"My lord." She tugged on her arm. Did the man fear Arabella so he was willing to make a scene?

The viscount looked to his nemesis and then quickly to Charlotte, a pleading expression on his face.

Ashton's eyes narrowed when he saw the viscount's arm gripping Charlotte's elbow, and he made a noise sounding suspiciously like a growl.

While she was flattered, she also wanted to diffuse the situation. "On second thought, Viscount Kernwith, would you mind fetching me some punch?"

Lord Kernwith released her. "Yes, but of course." He turned in all haste to leave.

Arabella stepped in front of Charlotte and called after the young lord. "Perhaps others would like a punch as well."

Viscount Kernwith half-turned and nodded.

"Whatever was that all about?" Ashton's smooth baritone was lined with control.

Charlotte leaned into him and whispered. "The lord and Arabella do not suit."

"Ah," and he was smart enough to leave it be. "Would you care for a turn about the garden, Mrs. Wold?"

"Yes, Major, that would be lovely."

Arabella pivoted toward them and scowled. "You can't go. Pierce has gone to retrieve refreshments for us."

"I am certain the major and I will return before Lord Kernwith arrives with refreshments," Charlotte assured her.

"And if we are not, the two of you may explore the gardens to find us," Ashton said with a glint in his eye.

Arabella nodded, her expression smooth.

When they were some distance away, Charlotte suppressed a giggle and said, "You are a wicked man."

"Madam, you have no idea." The glint in his eyes became fire as she stared into their dark forest depths.

"Oh, I suspect I might have some. I *was* married after all," she said as they crossed beneath the threshold.

"I was wondering if we would speak of it."

"I fear we must." Charlotte slowed her steps. "Amelia doesn't know Robert found me lacking."

"What?"

"He often left me alone rather than force his baser needs upon me." Charlotte blushed. Oh, the shame in admitting one's lack of allure. Did he see it? She hoped not. She didn't know what was wrong with her.

"Your marriage, it was, that is to say...You're not a... a... oh bloody hell." He ran a hand through his dark hair.

Since he struggled to speak, Charlotte assisted him. "Our marriage was consummated, but Robert was rather fond of his mistress in London."

His posture went rigid. "I beg your pardon?"

She wrung her hands. What would he think? "I'm just not certain why he had to see her."

"As a married woman, I'm certain you knew why he went there."

Charlotte's cheeks grew hot and it was her turn to stumble, "Well, yes, but..." What to say? She wanted to hit him for making her uncomfortable.

He chuckled.

She surrendered to her urges.

"Ow!" He rubbed his arm, just below the shoulder.

"I'm sorry, I'm not used to speaking of such wicked things."

He leaned close enough the hairs on the back of her neck rose when he spoke. "I can't imagine the late Reverend Wold abandoning you for a light skirt, let alone being wicked."

She couldn't imagine where the next words came from as she and the major turned to make their way to the garden. "Perhaps, *I* wanted to be the wicked one."

The next moment, she was lifted off the ground and ushered into the dark shadows. Her back flattened against the cold bricks.

"Do not tease me, Charlotte," Myles warned.

He doesn't think I am too forward. Once her relief subsided, the strength with which he lifted her radiated from his body to hers. She raised her head and gazed into his eyes. "I would never, Ashton."

He didn't speak. Instead, he stared at her for a moment, and then he pressed his lips to hers.

Dear Lord, she tasted like warm honey, Myles thought, his senses overwhelmed. Dazed for a moment, he broke the kiss, nuzzled her neck, and inhaled lavender. He recalled it from their night in the carriage. Her skin was smooth and supple. Her honeyed and intoxicating scent consumed him as it wafted to his nostrils. As he tasted her sweetness, his lust built. How could this woman think she was anything less than desirable?

He pulled her closer, his hands skimming the dark silk of her bodice wishing it were bare skin.

Soft laughter floated across the balcony like a douse of cold water.

Myles shoved Charlotte away from him. He looked to where the sounds were followed by people, but none entered the dark gardens.

When he turned back to Charlotte, she was once again tangled in the shrubbery. She weaved, grasping the bush leaves to steady herself.

"I am sorry." He reached to assist, but stopped, hand extended. If he touched her, he would be unable to stop himself from drawing her into his arms and kissing her soundly.

Having found her footing, she waved him off. "I am fine. You must cease this startling habit where I end up dazed and upon the ground." Though she sounded irritated and breathless, he found the combination and her imagery alluring and devastating to his control. He wasn't some untried youth, he was a man, a soldier. Control was how he managed day-to-day. Well, it wasn't a problem until he met this intoxicating siren!

Charlotte darted a glance toward the new arrivals and hastened toward him. "Take my arm," she instructed. He did. "Please return me to Lady Devonhold, and let me be." She was as cold as a Scottish winter morning.

He ran a hand through his hair. "Truly, I am sorry. I was trying to--"

"What! Myles?" Of course, she would use his given name when she was mad at him. "Save my reputation? Do not mistake me for some virginal debutante. After all, I *am* a widow."

"Dammit, Charlotte! What would you have me do?" Myles steered her deeper into the gardens. He refused to let her leave him angry.

"Nothing." Her lips flattened into a white slash.

"You're as stiff as a board, and a moment ago you..."

"What? I was about to let you have your way with me?" She folded her arms over her chest. The swells of her breasts pushed above her bodice.

How far would their kiss have gone? Myles steered her even further away from the house.

Charlotte's voice was a bit shrill as she spoke. "Look, Myles, I am not someone you toy with. Simply because I have more experience than a debutante doesn't mean you get to treat me like a... a... a..." She blushed and then gulped.

The combination was humorously adorable.

"...a common strumpet," she concluded.

Myles couldn't help it; he buckled over, laughing. Unable to resist her pull, he tried to draw her back into his arms.

Unable to resist her, he tried to draw her back into his arms, but she stomped on his foot. When he winced, she smiled in triumph. He stared at her. "I deserve your ire."

"You do." She was unapologetic.

Despite the sting in his left foot, he'd not been this distracted since returning to England.

"There is a bench over here." She offered him her arm. He waved her off as he limped toward the bench, and waited until she sat before seating himself. He turned to gaze at her in the darkness. "I am sorry, I—"

"Stop!" She raised her hand. "I do not want to hear your regrets for kissing me."

"I never regret kissing a beautiful woman." He shifted closer to her, so his thigh brushed against her silken skirt.

"Well, um, thank you." Charlotte stared at her lap.

He lifted her chin to meet his gaze. "You truly are, you know."

She gave him a small smile, revealing her enchanting dimples.

He swallowed hard. "I am tempted to kiss you again."

"What is stopping you?" Charlotte asked, leaning closer.

Chapter Six

But Myles pulled back slightly. "Forgive me, but I'd like to keep my other foot," said, rubbing the arch of his left foot, where she'd stepped on him.

"I'm sorry." Charlotte looked at his leg. "Does your injury still bother you?"

He shook his head. "Not physically. Though I didn't need it, I was lucky to have the cane. Not only is it good if I've been attacked by a kid slipper, but I can also use it in self-defense."

She swallowed hard before asking, "You've hurt people with it?"

"No reason to, as of yet. The uniform usually deters aggressors. I'll hate to see it go."

She whipped her head up. "You're leaving the army?"

Myles nodded. "I am. Since my uncle passed, I've inherited property in Scotland, and I want to settle down."

"So, you are looking for a bride." Charlotte scooted to the end of the bench, and Myles closed the gap between them again.

"Not at all. I wouldn't mind some companionship. Don't you get lonely?"

"No. Currently, I'm surrounded by your brother's family."

"I was wondering how you came to arrive here. Were you a governess at Lady Pittham's house?"

"No. After Robert died, I had nowhere to turn until I remembered Lord Devonhold's birthday party."

"And I had left right before. It seems as if we were destined to meet." She gave him a hard stare. "So you could have a wife?"

"Perhaps. Do you have any family?"

"My younger brother, Nigel, lives in London."

"So, why not stay with your brother?"

She laughed. "My brother is perpetually on tour. I haven't seen him since my wedding. I'm not certain he even has a home."

"What will you do, once our ruse is over?"

"You mean when you cry off?"

"Or you may?"

"I don't have a reputation that requires me to marry." Charlotte struggled to quell the burning sensation in her chest. "It no longer matters. Robert is dead, and I am here, but I'm not certain how long that will be."

"I could help you." He looked sincere. "I may have a position to offer you on my estate."

"Oh?"

"Yes, I have a young ward. My cousin. I'm not certain how old she is, but if she requires a governess, I would gladly give you the position."

Guests could be heard talking and walking along the path. Ashton put a respectable distance between them just before a couple moved past them. He raked a hand through his hair. "Although, perhaps such a temptation is not wise."

"Why are you offering me a position simply to remove it?" Charlotte willed herself to look at him.

He glanced away, perusing the shrubbery as if counting the individual leaves.

"I'm drawn to you, and since we first met, I have a memory of the beautiful determination in your face that I cannot seem to dispel."

She swiveled slowly, her head puzzled at this new thought. "You find me attractive. Truly?"

"Do not misunderstand me, Charlotte. I want you very much, painfully so. However, I am not in the habit of bedding women," he said with hushed force.

Charlotte turned back in surprise. She crossed her arms and tilted her head staring intensely at him. "Are *you* innocent?"

He laughed. The warm sound rippled through the air. Charlotte's fingers itched to touch him. "No. I mean, I do not bed women of quality."

She found his assessment of her fascinating. "You've never had a mistress?"

"I've never been in a position to offer carte blanche."

"So, you've only bedded..." Dare she say it? "Prostitutes?"

"And the occasional wid--" His mouth snapped shut.

"Ah, ha!" She pointed a finger at him. "Widow. You were going to say, 'widow.'"

"I was." His mouth curved upward and his green eyes glowed. He devastated her senses.

"Ashton, I *am* a widow." Why did she continue to pursue him? Like him, she should simply back away from temptation. But just once she wanted to feel loved, even if it was an illusion.

"Yes, of the late Reverend Wold." He frowned.

Charlotte exhaled. It would be best to leave him alone and abandon any pursuit of happiness, however brief. Her affection for him intensified in their short association. Yet such an attraction would be perilous. He believed her pious like her husband.

"I do not like to think of you married," he said in a clipped tone.

It was her turn to laugh. "Why ever not?"

He ran a hand through his sable hair. It was starting to stand on end. "I am not certain. Mind you, I certainly do not think of you as a debutante either."

"Thank God for small graces," she sighed. The last thing she wanted was for him to treat her as if she needed to be guarded against, well, him.

"I should offer you marriage, instead of this false engagement." He was blunt, and she found his honesty refreshing.

She shook her head. "I do not want marriage. Is it not our agreement to avoid the state of matrimony? You suggested we form an attachment, so our lovely friends do not marry us off."

He groaned heavily. "I suppose you are correct."

She scooted closer to him. "What if we modify our agreement?"

He remained on the bench and met her gaze head-on. "What did you have in mind?"

"I would not be averse to certain liberties." What was it about this man? She could not control her wicked tongue. She had made a lifelong habit of leaping from the fire into a wild river. *Why stop now?*

He stood. "Charlotte, I cannot."

She rose. As Myles observed, she was no debutante. Perhaps it was better he learned her true nature if they were to go on. She glared at him and placed her hands on her hips. "You kissed me! What is so wrong with me that you will not consider a mutually beneficial arrangement?"

"I *did* consider you! Without thinking, I took advantage of you. My actions were rude and callous." He rubbed the back of his neck.

"Was I not a willing participant?" She clenched her hands, resisting the urge to slap him for his sudden chivalry.

"I am not certain." His expression was pointed.

"Do you think your male prowess duped me? Or do you believe me so incapable of knowing my mind I cannot decide matters of the flesh?" She swallowed, lifted her chin, and boldly met his gaze.

"No." His body stiffened. She half expected him to salute.

"Well, it must be something! Why else would you reject a woman you find attractive? I am all but throwing myself at you." Her attraction and his indifference vexed her.

Charlotte was in high dudgeon at the moment. Her volatile nature should ward him off, yet she was desirable. Her skin flushed and her breasts rose and fell with each rapid breath. Her bodice threatened to expose more flesh with each inhale. His heart beat faster in her presence. One hour with her and he was more alive than he had been this past year.

"When you make up your mind, you know where to find me." She turned and rushed away in a huff.

Myles watched the swish of her dark skirt until the night enveloped her. Her slippers moved quietly along the stone until he was alone with only the soundless night. He gripped his cane with his left hand as he ambled back toward the house.

What was wrong with him? Was he some sort of muttonhead? Why didn't he chase after her? She was irresistible. His blasted impulses led him to this very argument. Was he such a bastard, he didn't care about her feelings or the consequences? He shook his head at his cowardice. He couldn't risk entanglement with her. Though he formulated a plan to be close to her, he did not dare let the gossip mongers bandy about simply to satisfy his needs.

The faint sound of movement caused his breath to hitch. The French doors on the balcony opened and closed. He looked toward them, expecting her return. Nothing. Cold sweat dampened his forehead. He shuffled back toward the ballroom. The celebration within remained fierce. Yet he stood alone.

Servants he didn't know tumbled from a nearby door. The maid straightened upon seeing him and the manservant bowed. "Sir."

Myles nodded. He needed a stiff drink. When he entered the ballroom, he immediately searched for Charlotte. To do what? He had no idea. Things between them were unfinished. Perhaps she was correct. He needed to sort himself. He strolled through the chaos until he found Viscount Kernwith staring into the card room, seemingly mystified.

"Kernwith!"

The viscount jumped upon hearing his name and turned. "Ashton. What do you want?"

"Have a drink with me." Even he heard the discontent in his voice.

"Why?" Kernwith eyed him suspiciously.

"Because a man shouldn't wallow alone." And Myles was in some serious need of wallowing because he had no idea what to do about his desire for Charlotte.

Kernwith nodded.

They made their way to James' study, winding past the wistful looks of the country ladies.

Myles cracked the heavy chestnut door, and peered in, relieved to find the room empty. He slipped in. Kernwith followed. Myles retrieved the good scotch from behind the desk, along with two glasses. He poured a dram into each glass.

"What are you wallowing in?" Kernwith retrieved his tumbler off the desk.

"What else? A woman."

"The Widow Wold?"

"What other woman is there?" Myles drank the amber liquid. It tasted sour and did nothing to numb him. He discharged another.

"There are many women available this weekend. Why the widow? Let her go, and choose another chit." Kernwith raised his glass before taking a drink.

"I suggest you heed your advice. I've seen the way you stare at Arabella." Myles pointed sternly at him.

"We have a tangled past."

"Best you be more specific, Kernwith, or I'll have to ask for pistols at dawn." Myles set his glass down. "Miss Kendall is, after all, my sister."

Kernwith's brows drew together and his features tightened. "Only by marriage, you bastard."

Myles shrugged unaffected by the label. "It takes one to know one."

"Touché." Kernwith took another drink.

"What is your relationship with Arabella?" Though he was only half-kidding about calling Kernwith out, he did feel a certain responsibility toward his extended family.

"It's nothing untoward, I assure you." Kernwith stared straight ahead, though he didn't meet Myles' gaze. "What about the widow Wold?"

"Complicated." He couldn't very well reveal his awareness to Charlotte without revealing his less-than-noble thoughts.

"I see. She's demanding marriage and all before she assumes the role of a merry widow?" Kernwith finished his drink and set the empty glass on the desk.

"Do not say such things about her. She's *not* demanding marriage. As I said, it is complicated."

"Sounds like you are the one complicating it." Kernwith stood, turned, and strode toward the door.

Myles had no answer. He *was* complicating it. He wanted to marry her, not because he loved her, but simply because after tonight he couldn't imagine his life without her. He simply needed to persuade her. A monumental task indeed. She'd been the one to ask for more during their time together, and he'd rejected her. She had given him the perfect tool to compromise her until she came to her senses. "God, I *am* an idiot."

"I'll leave you to wallow in peace." Kernwith raised his glass and hastened through the door.

With a loud click, the barrier was closed and Myles was once again alone in a house full of guests.

Chapter Seven

Sunlight filtered into the room. Charlotte turned away from the window and burrowed further beneath the covers. Charlotte moaned, even her voice hurt. She didn't feel like climbing from her bed. After Ashton's rejection, she'd gone to the card room with Arabella, Amelia, and Lady Worthington. She'd stayed awake, eaten, and imbibed in far too much sherry.

Once she retreated to her room last evening, she tossed and turned in a wretched fit. Her eyes ached as if they'd been washed with sand, and her limbs were bone-weary.

The door opened, followed by light footsteps and whistling. The soft noises grated along her scalp.

"Are you awake, Mrs. Wold?" Lizzy asked.

"Unfortunately, yes," Charlotte mumbled into the pillow.

"I brought one of Lady Fitzwilliam's riding habits for today's adventure." Lizzy's cheerful voice was like shards of glass to Charlotte's temples.

"Riding habit?"

"Yes, there is a picnic planned at the gazebo on the far end of the property." The excitement in the maid's voice forced Charlotte to throw the covers over her head. She had forgotten Amelia's scheduled outing to entertain the couples. On top of the current guests, Lady Worthington's sons were expected to arrive this morning as well.

Charlotte groaned.

"You've missed breakfast, so I took the liberty of having Cook prepare a tray."

"Thank you, Lizzy." Honestly, anything to avoid facing Amelia, Lady Worthington, and whomever else was involved in the miserable matchmaking schemes. To think, she had marveled at Ashton's brilliant solution. Yet, in one breath, he'd gone from seduction to rejection. The man infuriated her. Once their dissociation was public, efforts to see her down the aisle would increase two-fold. Ashton's second thoughts and Amelia's matchmaking were more than anyone should endure. She couldn't stay forever at Devonhold, and yet she required a better solution, not a wretched husband. Was this simple request too much to ask?

A knock on the door broke through Charlotte's ill-conceived plans.

"That'll be your breakfast, Mrs. Wold." Lizzy's joy was nearly infectious. The maid's unfiltered sunny disposition threatened to chase away her dark mood.

The pièce de résistance was the scent of warm cinnamon along with hints of black tea which finally beckoned Charlotte from the bed.

Lizzy handed her a robe before pouring the tea and readying the tray.

Charlotte shuffled along the cold wooden floor toward the round table where the tray had been set. She tightened the sash before seating herself. Her hands wrapped around the cup, the warmth from the porcelain permeating her fingers and traveling along her limbs, while the aromatic steam tickled her nose. She took a tentative sip and sighed.

"Well, Mrs. Wold, what do you think?" Lizzy approached her with the riding habit Amelia sent.

Like the gown she'd worn last night, this too was from Amelia's wardrobe. Charlotte recalled the habit from last Season, or perhaps the one previous. The twill fabric was a grayish blue reminiscent of a sky laden with heavy rain. She gave a most unladylike snort.

"Do you not care for it? I can send it back." Lizzy's eyes held a look of panic.

"No. No. No. It is fine. I am sorry, my mind was elsewhere."

Lizzy gave an audible sigh.

Charlotte twisted the end of the ties. She hadn't meant to cause the maid such worry. "Lizzy."

"Yes, Mrs. Wold."

"You may call me Charlotte."

"If you insist, Miss Charlotte." Lizzy's voice held hesitation, or perhaps she was simply testing the new name.

Charlotte didn't bother to correct her. "I want you to know, you have taken excellent care of me. If I appear in any way not content, please know it is not your service. I am simply unused to such luxuries."

Lizzy nodded and went about preparing the habit while Charlotte ate her breakfast. "Miss Charlotte?"

"Yes, Lizzy."

"If I may be so bold?"

Give the girl an inch. "I would never punish boldness, Lizzy."

"Are you looking to get remarried? Perhaps to Major Ashton?"

Oh dear, the servants were already gossiping. Charlotte paused before responding. "I am not certain if I am meant for such a blessed union." Charlotte shivered. "I wasn't very good at it."

Lizzy's face scrunched up. "How is one good at marriage?"

"The late Reverend Wold was very disappointed in me. He found me lacking." Charlotte knew better than to speak of such things to a servant, but she couldn't stop the words from bubbling forth.

Lizzy frowned. "Beg your pardon Miss Charlotte, but the man must have been a dunderhead. You're quite lovely and from my point of view, very kind. Not many in your position would speak to those of us less than."

It was Charlotte's turn to frown. "Less than?"

"Less than our betters."

"What utter nonsense! Lizzy, the vagaries of fate are the only thing standing between you and me."

"How so?"

"Are you aware I am of the middling class?"

"I..."

"My father was a vicar, much like my late husband. I should not have married a man who I knew lived on the whims of others. Had I not remembered Lady Devonhold's invitation to come and visit, I would have had to either return to my parents or fend for myself. Even now I am considering all available options."

"Are you not a governess to the Misses Prudence and Magdalene?"

"Yes, but they are grown and ready for their Seasons. They no longer need me."

"Perhaps you could serve as their chaperone," Lizzy offered.

"Perhaps." A chaperone position would likely bring her into contact with the London Season, but a governess position tickled her and was a far better option than returning to her father's tyrannical doorstep. Perhaps she could find a governess position in the countryside, where most parents were content to leave their offspring at the estate until children reached a certain age.

"Are you an only child?" Lizzy asked.

"I have a brother, Nigel, but he is traveling abroad." For a man of little means, her brother lived a life of luxury. He'd been traveling since he'd left home two years ago. Nigel always thought he was better than his roots, spending time and money in gambling halls, bawdy houses, and away from home and responsibilities. Nigel might not welcome her with open arms, but it was worth a try. "Lizzy, you are a genius!"

"I am?"

"Yes, you are. Please apologize to Lady Devonhold for my tardiness. I must send a letter to my brother." She had no idea where her brother was in the world. She would post it to his solicitor. At least the letter would prevent her from having to settle for a husband, no matter how suitable Major Ashton may be.

Dear Nigel,

I haven't heard from you in ages, but desperately require your assistance. My time as a governess for the Devonhold estate is coming to an end. I do not desire to enter the Marriage Mart at this stage in my life. My only current offer is for that of a mistress at a country estate in Scotland. If I do not hear from you, I may be forced to accept.

Sincerely,

Your sister, Charlee

Charlotte couldn't help but smile. That ought to encourage her brother to acknowledge her.

Myles looked again at the main house. Though the weather was nowhere near warm he unbuttoned his coat and loosened his cravat. Where was she?

Amelia shouted from the carriage. "Let us get underway."

"Where's Charlotte?" he couldn't keep from asking.

All eyes turned to him.

Joan, seated opposite Amelia, leaned out the window and scolded him. "Ashton, where is your sense of propriety!"

Heat rose along his neck. Myles was well aware of his *faux pas*. "Forgive me. I merely wanted to ensure all parties were present."

His newly arrived nephews, David—the heir—and Daniel—the spare—Worthington started snickering.

Amelia frowned at him. "Charlotte is penning a letter to be sent post-haste. She assured me she will follow as soon as possible."

Viscount Kernwith spoke up, "I can wait for the Widow Wold."

"Unnecessary, my good man. I shall stay behind," Myles insisted. He was determined to straighten out this havoc alone.

Viscount Kernwith shrugged.

Myles waited as the carriage full of ladies and the men following on horseback meandered down the drive. Once the party disappeared from his vision, he dismounted and made rapid strides toward the stables. He was startled to find Charlotte there.

"Charlotte," he sighed.

She turned. "Major." Her voice was chilly.

His breath caught and he found himself at a loss. Charlotte was lovelier each time he laid his eyes upon her. She wore a gray riding habit matching her eyes, making them more pronounced on her elfin face. A blue feather from her cap teased her cheekbones, reminding Myles of her soft skin. "I waited for you."

"Do not do me any favors." She turned back as the groom prepared her mount, a gray whose markings complemented Charlotte's habit.

"I am sorry."

She twirled about and faced him with her hands on her hips. A storm brewed in her eyes. "Do not bother apologizing. Too much regret lacks sincerity, and with your quick about-face, you'll end up overeating humble pie."

Her words crashed into him like a lightning bolt. "I was an ass," he confessed.

Her mouth tipped up in the corners. "I am listening."

Stepping closer to her, he lowered his voice, lest the groom eavesdropped. "You were right. I shouldn't have implied there was anything untoward in a physical relationship between us. The truth of the matter is I desire you very much."

Her eyes widened. "I find you attractive as well."

Myles rose to the occasion and shifted uncomfortably.

Charlotte lowered her gaze. Her pink tongue darted out, licking her lower lip.

"Stop that," he growled.

Her eyes fluttered to his face, and if not for the gleam in her silvery eyes he may have believed her innocent. "I am sure I do not know what you mean."

Oh, if they were alone. He began to imagine just that. This woman was tempting and certainly worth giving her his name. First, he had to show her how good they could be together and that a marriage of convenience was the best course of action. Yet she offered herself up on a platter. Perhaps if she didn't see reason he should show her the benefits of a union. "Shall we join the others?"

"Certainly."

Myles let the groom assist her with her mount. As enticing as it might be to lift and lay his hands upon her form, his lingering touch would fuel the gossip, and servants were the worst.

They set out at a steady pace on horseback, rounding the bend where the group had disappeared from his sight.

"You seat a horse well," he said.

"Thank you. I've been riding since I was a child. I learned from Amelia and Arabella."

"Oh, I wasn't aware Amelia rode."

"Their father taught them, as he found it a useful skill."

"He taught them to ride sidesaddle?"

She giggled. "No. He taught them to ride astride."

"You can ride astride?" His voice was thick and unsteady.

She gave him a wicked stare. "I am quite adept at it."

His front falls were snug. The image of her riding him was now seared into his mind. He struggled with his next question. "What other skills do you possess?"

"Domestically or otherwise?"

He coughed. "Both?"

A slow secret smile crossed her features before she answered. "Well, as a once middling miss myself, I can cook in a pinch."

"I'm impressed." He was. He tried to imagine his sister doing anything remotely domestic and cringed at the image his mind produced.

She must have misinterpreted his expression. "It's nothing like Amelia's chef prepares but it serves passably well. My mother had higher aspirations for me, hence I learned to read, write, and do arithmetic."

"Truly?"

She nodded. "In addition to this foundation, I speak French, mastered the domestic arts, and even had time to touch a needle to fabric. I have all the skills a young lady of the realm might require."

"What aspirations did your mother have?" Her training and pedigree were perfect for him.

"She hoped I might marry above my station. Much like Amelia. Thank God Amelia and Lord Devonhold wed after I had made my marriage bed."

"And did marriage agree with you?" Although he didn't want to hear how wonderful the late Reverend Wold may have been, he wanted to know more about Charlotte.

Her horse threw its head from side to side. She reined it in before answering. "Perhaps it would have been more palatable if I hadn't rushed headlong into it."

"Perhaps it was your choice of husband." Why had Charlotte married a man who had not seen fit to treat her properly? When Myles married, and the idea appealed to him more and more, he would never stray.

"Reverend Wold certainly didn't improve our union." Her face held a pinched expression.

"So your parents arranged a marriage with a man of the cloth. It seems odd if they trained you as you say."

"You misunderstand, Major. I eloped without my parents' consent." Her mouth turned downward.

"Your husband swept you off your feet?" Bile rose within him as he asked about a man loose in the haft.

"He was a means to an end."

"Tell me."

"I'd rather not speak of it." Her lips compressed, and her gray eyes were blue as storm clouds filled with rain.

They rode the remainder of the way in silence before joining the others.

Charlotte greeted Amelia and the Kendall sisters warmly. Their presence helped her avoid looking at Ashton. She was more attracted to him than to any other man here, or any she had met before him. What would it be like to be with such a man?

"Did you send off your letter?" Amelia asked after they had enjoyed their picnic.

"Yes. It should arrive in a few days. Hopefully, Nigel will reply, and I may reside with him." Charlotte caught Ashton's sidelong glance at her.

His look was intent and... curious?

"Are you certain you want to?" Amelia's voice was cautious.

"I cannot stay here forever."

"I thought you and Myles—"

"I am not certain what Major Ashton wants, but it certainly is *not* me." Even Charlotte was shocked by the derision in her voice.

Amelia bristled.

Lady Worthington chimed in. "We can find you a well-intentioned man."

"David and Daniel have arrived," Amelia shot back.

"Lady Fitzwilliam! My sons are—"

"Far too young for me," Charlotte spoke before Lady Worthington could complete a sentence most likely ending in an insult.

"Just so. Mrs. Wold requires a more established gentleman. I've taken the liberty of inviting your neighbor, Sir John. He is also recently widowed, having lost his wife to..."

"Old age." Amelia interrupted. "Christ, Joan! He's nearly as old as Charlotte's father."

She was almost afraid to ask, as she'd never met Sir John. "How old is he?"

"Admiral Fridley recently celebrated his sixty-second birthday. A lonely one, I might add, since his wife's passing eight months ago," Lady Worthington said half-aloud in response. Apparently established meant old as the hills.

"Doesn't Sir Fridley require an heir?" Amelia pressed.

Lady Worthington waved a hand. "Nonsense. He has a daughter who could inherit his extensive empire, should she marry properly."

"I suppose you have a bridegroom selected for her. Perhaps David?" Amelia asked.

Lady Worthington blinked rapidly. "*Not* David. He is the future Marquess of Worthington. I would want someone of better breeding than the Fridley girl."

To include me. Was she truly destined to be *only* a wife? What a dull existence. She would speak with Amelia. Perhaps searching for a posting as a governess would be beneficial in the event her brother would not come up to snuff.

"I've heard Admiral Fridley keeps a mistress in Brighton," Prudence interjected.

"And a base-born child, no less," Lady Worthington supplied. "I wonder if Major Ashton is familiar with Fridley's by-blow?"

"Do you assume all bastards know each other?" Charlotte couldn't refrain from asking. However, not before she'd noticed the men moved on ahead and out of earshot.

"Perhaps, Mrs. Wold, you aren't cultured enough for Admiral Fridley," Lady Worthington huffed.

"I believe it best we return." Amelia, always the peacekeeper, spoke before Charlotte could respond. It was just as well. Charlotte wanted nothing to do with the elderly Admiral Fridley.

"The skies do look as if they threaten to open, do they not?" Prudence stated.

Lady Worthington and the Kendall girls returned to the safety of their carriage and Charlotte let the footman assist her with her mount, but she lingered at the edge of the green.

Amelia leaned out from the window. "Are you coming, Charlotte?"

"I'll be with you in a bit. I shall be back before dinner," she assured her friend.

"We will see you then. Ride along, Stewart." Amelia shouted at the coachman.

The carriage rolled back to the house. Once the ladies left her line of vision, she rode toward the border between Sir John's property and the Devonhold Estate. Following along the remains of a crumbling stone wall patched in spots with wood, she realized she would miss riding in the country when she went to live with her brother. Perhaps he had access to horses? Maybe she could ride in Hyde Park, but it wasn't quite the same. The air in the country was fresher, the sky bluer and she was free.

Charlotte huffed to herself. She hadn't had the opportunity to enjoy rides while married to Robert. Along with his many other faults, the man had been a miser, hoarding every shilling. His asceticism was part of the reason Charlotte arrived with so few belongings. She had made do with fewer new gowns and habits. Even sleeping without a night rail, huddled in her bed cold and alone.

Charlotte's musings about her wardrobe halted as the light mist gave way to rather heavy rain. She turned her horse around, not knowing exactly where she was, but understanding most horses had an inane sense to find their way home, or the nearest building resembling such.

Her mare struggled up a hilly slope along the fence line, and halfway up the horse lost its footing and slid back toward the riverbank. The mare's rump dropped, and the beast wrongly assumed Charlotte was the problem.

The horse panicked, throwing her haunches upward in a buck to dislodge her rider.

Charlotte held the reins, but the horse continued fighting.

Once at the bottom near the bank, and before the gray did something stupid, as horses were prone, Charlotte resigned to lead the frightened horse up the muddy bank. She slipped loose of the saddle, seeking to find firm ground with her boots. But the horse...

The horse, noticing a weight reduction found its footing and bolted in the direction of the stable.

The momentum propelled Charlotte backward into the stream. Her last thought before she landed was wondering why on earth she missed riding such stupid animals.

Chapter Eight

Myles waited at the stables for Charlotte. What was the woman doing? Nearly an hour had passed since the ladies' carriage had arrived. For the past quarter-hour, rain fell in sheets. Yet, no one asked about Charlotte's whereabouts. Was he the only one who cared? Correction, Myles was *concerned*. He didn't *care*. How could he? He hadn't known Charlotte long enough. He was merely trying to deduce what had happened. Or so he tried to convince himself.

Before he could question his unexplained apprehension, the gray mare that Charlotte had ridden earlier sauntered into the stable—without Charlotte.

The groom grabbed the mare's reins.

Myles' agitation overrode his sense of propriety, and he exited the stables calling, "Charlotte! Charlotte!" In the short time he'd been outside in the elements, his clothes were drenched. He marched back to where the groom was currently rubbing the horse down. "Mrs. Wold has not returned."

"Perhaps she be at the house," the groom hypothesized.

"And not return her horse?"

The groom merely shrugged and went back to tending the gray mare. "Who knows what these pampered birds, er, ladies think."

"Ready my horse and send someone to the house to confirm Mrs. Wold's whereabouts."

"Sir, there be no sense in saddling Ares if the lady be at the house," the groom grumbled.

"Regardless, I am going riding, whether the widow is in Devonhold or not."

As if sensing his master's restlessness, Ares stomped in his stall.

The groom, distracted by the noise, loosened his grip on the mare's reins, and she darted for the nearest entrance. The groom stood dumbfounded facing the doorway the gray had exited.

Ares reared, pulling on the rope which held him to the outside wall. He shifted, rotated, and kicked his back feet, cracking the stall's walnut sides.

Myles strode over to Ares. "Well old boy, do you want to find the gray?"

Ares snorted, the air from the horse's nostrils puffed like steam. The chilled air outside had seeped into the structure.

"All right, boy." Myles unwound the slip knot and grabbed Ares' bridle. He quickly haltered the horse and mounted him.

"Sir, you do not have a saddle!" the groom protested.

"I wouldn't want to inconvenience you," Myles shouted behind him as Ares stampeded after the mare, who would hopefully lead him to Charlotte.

Myles surrendered hope as the mare led Ares on a wild chase right back to the stables. He stayed mounted while the groom tethered the mare then he and Ares rode out once again. They rode to where the ladies had enjoyed tea on their outing, but she was not there.

The ground was a muddy mess, so it was impossible to see any tracks. He decided to follow the border wall between the Devonhold and Forestrong Estate, now owned by Admiral Fridley or Sir John, as Joan called him.

As they neared the stream, Ares spooked and reared. Myles held his seat and calmed the horse down. Once he surveyed the hillside, he learned why the horse startled. He'd never seen a more beautiful and relieving sight.

Charlotte was making her way up the hill, her habit caked in mud. Since she was barely discernible as human, it was no wonder his horse was spooked. Wet and mud-laden, Ashton could see each step was a battle as she struggled to find her footing.

"Hello!" he shouted over the rain.

She scowled up at him as he approached. Her face, hair, and clothes were wet and plastered against her form. They were laden down with water and soil as well, only her wide gray eyes identified her as his Charlotte.

"I fear you may have to take them off." He nodded to her skirts.

A look of horror crossed her face. "What?"

"Your skirts." He dismounted and tied Ares to the fence border at the top of the incline.

She frowned at him. "I am not getting naked for your perverse pleasure, Ashton."

Myles smiled, relieved she reverted to his surname and not the chilly title of major. Myles cautiously navigated his way toward Charlotte. He held onto the fence for fear he too would fall into similar circumstances.

Once he reached her, he clarified, "You do not have to remove all your clothing. You simply need to remove your skirts."

Charlotte gave him a skeptical look.

"They are weighing and dragging you down. Besides, you could catch a cold."

She crossed her arms and promptly fell forward, planting her face on the soggy hill. He tried to catch her, but mud and momentum landed him on his backside. Charlotte raised herself on her hands, gaped at him, and then burst out laughing. Her laugh rippled through the air, warming him through the rain that had slowed once again to a mist.

Myles laughed with her.

"I need to be able to stand to remove this mud-covered skirt and the petticoats. So far, this problem has contributed to my struggle," Charlotte said.

"Here, take my hand." He thrust his left hand toward her, and she gripped him like a lifeline.

He wound his right arm around the wooden fence pole patching the worn ruins. "Ready?"

She nodded.

He tugged on her with all his strength, inch by inch, he pulled until he finally held a muddy and smiling Charlotte in his arms. "Are you ready to stand?"

"Yes."

"Hold the fence post here."

She did.

Myles pulled himself up. Once standing he asked, "Ready?"

"Please."

He hauled her against the fence line.

They stood face to face, and she was so beautiful he leaned in to kiss her.

"No!" Charlotte threw a hand up, mud flying towards him.

Myles ducked.

"We've made so much progress extracting myself from this muck, I do not dare risk it," she said.

He nodded.

"Turn around," she told him.

He raised an eyebrow.

"I am *not* undressing in front of you." She scowled.

Myles nodded and slowly turned around. He faced uphill and a very agitated Ares stared back shaking his head from side to side, before backing up as if trying to determine what creature Myles was conspiring with.

"You may look now," Charlotte said in a low and clear voice.

He did and what greeted him was perhaps the most bizarrely desirable woman he'd ever laid eyes on.

Charlotte wore her jacket over the top of her chemise and other underthings. Her feet were bare. He gave her a pointed look. "What?" she asked.

"No shoes?"

"The mud sucked them off my feet hours ago. The earth can keep them," she blew out the words.

"If you please, grab me about the waist after I turn around and we'll make our way up this hill."

"Yes, sir." She saluted him, flinging mud onto her forehead.

He shook his head and considered wiping it off, but to what point? He turned and began his dogged march up the hill, dragging Charlotte behind him like the most precious (and bedraggled) load of desirable femininity he'd ever laid eyes on. Once they topped the hill, he placed his jacket over her shoulders. He also removed his breeches and handed them to her, before putting his muddy hessians back on.

"What are you doing?" She asked.

"These garments are mostly dry, and I don't want you catching a cold." He gave her a curt nod and shoved them in her hands. Though it did nothing to hide his exposed legs, it would warm her.

Once she donned them, she looked adorable swimming in his jacket and breeches.

Areseyed Charlotte with suspicion but allowed Myles to lift her and place her on his back. Myles mounted behind her.

During their ride to Devonhold, he couldn't help holding her close, both for fear she would slip from the mount and because he wanted to. It seemed right to hold her. By the time they reached the estate, the sun decided to grace their presence. The fickle star also gave those gathered on the front steps a clear and unobstructed view of their entrance up the drive.

All hell broke loose when he returned with Charlotte in her state of undress.

Of course, NOW they gathered to look for the missing Charlotte.

Charlotte could barely hear herself think above the din of voices shouting as she and the Major rode toward the house.

"Ashton!" Lady Worthington fumed. "You are a rogue of the first order! Your scandalous behavior confirms my suspicions regarding your lack of character."

"Myles, how could you? You've compromised poor Charlotte. How will you repair the damage?" Amelia said as if all hopes were dashed.

If possible, Ashton held her closer.

"He did not. He saved me from drowning in the mud!" Charlotte protested. Why was everyone leaping to judgment? Especially in matters that did not concern them.

"Charlotte," Amelia implored. "Do not defend him! He is duty-bound to offer for you now."

"Oh for heaven's sake." Charlotte threw up her hands and wobbled on Aries' back, the mud not yet dry. "I am hardly a blushing maiden."

Lady Worthington interrupted what was sure to be a row between two friends. "Perhaps, we should discuss this indoors, after Mrs. Wold is attired more appropriately."

The younger Kendall sisters giggled, and the Dowling brothers snickered.

Charlotte took stock of her appearance and attire. Lady Worthington was correct, there was no reason to fuel further gossip. Charlotte's cheeks flushed. Proper indignation was replaced by true embarrassment.

"Ignore them, Charlotte," Ashton whispered in her ear. His voice gave her comfort and strength. She needed both if she was to survive this new obstacle her friends placed before her.

Amelia, as if finally noticing her friend's state of dress, and all the witnesses, began shooing the onlookers into the house. "Come along now. We need not observe any more of this business."

Lady Worthington followed suit. "David! Daniel! Go along. You both know this is not a subject for other ears."

Charlotte believed Lady Worthington would keep her sons from gossiping outside the family. She wished she held the same faith in Amelia's ability to rein in her sisters.

Once she and Ashton were alone, he dismounted. He placed his hands about her waist and effortlessly lifted her down. "I am so very sorry."

"It's not your fault. I should've returned sooner when I noticed the ground beneath my mare softened." She gripped his pants against her waist and shook her head at her foolishness.

"Nonetheless, I fear I must make an offer for you."

She raised her head and stared, startled by his suggestion. "What makes you think I desire it?"

"It does not matter. We are truly ensnared." He shrugged his broad shoulders.

"No. I have already freed myself from one man and his whims. I am not ready to leap into the arms of another." Her skin began to itch beneath his breeches, and a dull ache sunk into her limbs as she struggled against the black stillness in her mind.

"What happened?" His hands gripped her upper arms and a line of worry in his brow marred his handsome face.

Charlotte shook off his touch and her melancholy. She had already revealed too much. "Nothing you need to concern yourself over." She proceeded to slip away from him.

"Charlotte."

She stopped. She would not turn around and look at his wet shirt and bare thighs.

"When I make you mine, I will concern myself with your past, your safety, and most, of all, you."

That was misguided chivalry speaking. She doubted he wanted anything as permanent as a wife. Charlotte pulled his borrowed clothes tighter, hoping to hide her exposure from his perceptive stare before escaping to the safety of the manor.

Chapter Nine

As soon as he crossed the threshold, James whirled to face him. "Well, what do you have to say for yourself?"

"Regarding?"

"Do not be obtuse! You know very well I speak of the widow Wold. I told you not to bed her--"

"Stop! I have not bedded Charlotte." What had possessed him to have her take off her skirt? At the time, his actions were logical and necessary.

As well as an opportunity to covet a woman whom you cannot have.

"Charlotte, is it?" Lord Worthington's voice grated as he asked from a shadowed corner.

"What in blazes is *he* doing here?" Myles asked James, then turned to Worthington. "This is a family matter."

"My wife *is* your family." Lord Worthington scowled. "I am looking after her interests."

"What does she have to do with me?"

"Not a blessed thing, thank God. But, for whatever reason, Lady Worthington has chosen to take an interest in Mrs. Wold. I do not give a damn if you bed or wed the widow. Your relationship matters not a whit to me." Lord Worthington inspected his fingernails as if bored with the whole ordeal.

"So *why* are you here?" Myles paced the room.

"I am reporting whatever is decided back to my wife, so she doesn't embroil herself further in a potential scandal," Lord Worthington stated.

He was losing control of the situation. "Fine. Sit in your corner and be silent," Myles commanded.

Lord Worthington snorted and crossed his arms.

"You've stuck your foot in it this time, Myles." James shook his head.

"For God's sake, your picnic party abandoned the woman to the elements! I was the only one who went looking for her," Myles argued.

"Why?" asked Lord Worthington.

"I told you to be silent." Myles pinched the bridge of his nose.

"This isn't the army, Ashton, and I am not one of your soldiers," Worthington stated.

"Such a pity," Myles mumbled. The idea of ejecting the shadowed lord from the study in a very un-officer-like manner held appeal.

"Why did you go looking for her?" James asked.

"Why didn't you?" Myles maintained an even tone despite his heartbeat pounding in his ears.

James rested his hands on his hips. "We would have, had we been informed."

"I sent the groom to inform you." Myles stared agape.

"I never received word." James narrowed his eyes.

"Speak to your groom, then." Myles crossed his arms over his chest.

"I will. Back to the matter at hand. Do you intend to make an offer for the widow Wold?"

"I already did."

"And?"

"She hasn't given me an answer."

"There you have it, Devonhold! The woman has a decision to make. I'll inform Lady Worthington at once." Lord Worthington rose and moved as quickly as a messenger away from the front lines.

Myles was impressed and relieved the bombardment of questions ceased.

Before the door clicked shut, Cobb entered. "A message for Major Ashton, sir."

Myles grabbed the envelope from the butler's trembling hand and opened it post haste.

"What is it?" James asked.

"It's from Galahad, the butler at Mosswin Castle. He says I need to come post-haste as there is trouble with a neighboring lord and the women of the house." Myles folded the note and held it tightly in his fist.

"Women of the house?"

"I assume Galahad means Uncle Edgar's mistress and her daughter."

"From one scandal to another, eh?" His brother chuckled.

"So it would seem." Because of his sinful birth, Myles strove to avoid scandal. Now, he found himself in the thick of it.

"First you must resolve this business with the widow Wold," James said.

"Do not worry. I'll make an honest woman of her." Somehow, his vision of marriage didn't feel as crushing as it once had. He was attracted to Charlotte, and beyond their bed games, he anticipated they would carry on nicely.

"I will inform Amelia, so she can plan a wedding."

"Can you not wait until Charlotte has consented to marry me?" Myles ignored the mocking voice inside which insisted Charlotte might not agree to be his bride.

"Fine. But I will inform my wife of your intentions if for no other reason than to keep peace in my house. God forbid our sister knows something my wife does not." James shook his head.

Myles would propose in earnest this evening. He only hoped he could convince Charlotte of the virtues of marriage. Or perhaps he still needed to convince himself.

Charlotte sank deeper into the tub. She'd bothered the kitchen staff below to rinse her hair and face before her ablutions, rather than muddy the hot water they brought up. If she was taking a bath, she planned to enjoy it, rather than soak in water the color of charcoal. The notion reminded her of the gown she planned to wear this very evening. She'd told Amelia in no uncertain terms she was done borrowing clothes. After having to discard such fine garments this afternoon, she didn't want to be indebted to her friend any more than necessary.

Amelia meant well, but this was too much. The plans to ensure she was well dressed and presentable rubbed her wrong as if they were disguising some defect. All efforts in some grand scheme to see her down the aisle. Did every woman desire to marry? Charlotte recalled her youth when she had indeed desired marriage. How could she not? Her father was a tyrant of the first order and her mother viewed her daughter as an instrument for advancement. Her troubles began before Robert. Before she knew the evil of men, or rather, one particular man.

Her dark musings were interrupted by Lizzy's tell-tale jaunty whistling. Charlotte sank deeper into the tub.

"Good evening, Miss," Lizzy greeted.

"Hello, Lizzy."

"I understand you'll be wearing something from your wardrobe this evening." Lizzy flitted toward the bureau holding Charlotte's scant belongings.

"Yes, I have a gray gown I acquired shortly before Reverend Wold's death." Charlotte leaned forward to confirm Lizzy picked the correct garment. To this day, Charlotte wasn't sure what prompted the purchase. Robert certainly wouldn't have approved. Perhaps fate had known her husband wasn't long for the world.

"Oh, yes. This is lovely," Lizzy paused. "And sturdy. I can see this dress suits you."

"Thank you."

Lizzy came toward her. "Miss Charlotte, I'll help you wash your hair. I'll be but a moment to-- Dear Lord!"

Before Charlotte could sink back in the tub, the damage had been done. Lizzy had seen her back. The maid had glimpsed the faint scars which crisscrossed in a pattern outlining her supposed sins and spoke volumes larger than Lizzy's shock. Her father was a firm believer in 'Spare the rod. Spoil the child.' Her mother had been compliant but made certain her father never left scars anywhere others might see. Heaven forbid anyone know the true nature of the town vicar!

"Miss Charlotte, I... I..."

"Lizzy, you are correct. I could use some help washing my hair." She prayed the maid would take the hint and leave her discovery alone.

"Yes, Miss," Lizzy said before beginning the task of washing Charlotte's hair.

"And, Lizzy?" The maid stopped. Charlotte wasn't sure if the girl still breathed. "I'd rather you not speak of what you've seen here.

"I won't say a word," Lizzy promised.

Chapter Ten

Silence and furtive glances cast a pall on dinner, and as soon as his brother and Amelia stood, Myles rose from his chair. He caught Charlotte's sleeve and steered her into the garden before she could protest.

Charlotte was radiant this evening, and he recognized the gown as the color she had worn when they first met. Though the dress fit better, it was slightly faded. Yet, the dove gray gown was more suited to her than some of the more extravagant gowns and now discarded habits she'd borrowed. Charlotte's hair was unadorned and still damp from what he was sure was an intensive cleansing, given how the mud had frosted her like a baker's cake earlier. Imagining her in the tub caused a tightening in his breeches. She could not say yes soon enough.

If you are married to her, you can have her whenever and wherever you wish, including the tub.

"We should get married!" he blurted.

She stopped. "What?"

He fixed her with a stare. She was... shocked... no... irritated. "I propose we marry."

She shook her head. "Ashton," she sighed and rested a hand on his arm. "We have a perfectly good ruse. Why would you want to spoil it with actual matrimony?"

"Given what happened this afternoon, I'm not certain we have a choice."

She frowned. "I don't believe anyone will say anything."

"Then you are being naïve," he said bluntly. "I'm afraid I must insist. As much as I hate to agree with her, Joan was correct - you are compromised." A deep part of him wanted her and did not care by what means necessary.

"I am not some innocent person who requires the good intentions of Lady Worthington or Amelia."

"I know."

"Then why are you insisting?"

"I must admit, I find you more fascinating than any woman of my past, and I desire you." He clenched his jaw as silent moments passed before she spoke.

"Please understand, I do not want to marry *anyone*."

The sadness, no, fear in her eyes was almost enough to halt him.

Seeing the change on her face, he wanted to put all the pieces together. "What happened, Charlotte?"

Biting her lip, she looked away. "It's not of import."

"It is. Our marriage could stand between you and happiness." Myles couldn't believe the words bursting from his mouth. Marriage was not something he conceived of until Charlotte. She was bringing about changes in him.

"Why are you concerned about my happiness? You do not have to get married. You have an estate that requires your attention. Do you not?"

"Well, yes. However, it is wrong to leave things unsettled between us."

Her smooth brow furrowed. "And your solution is we marry?"

"Yes." The more he considered a lifetime with this woman, the more he liked the idea of her by his side. Even with his ward and her mother on the Mosswin estate, he imagined it would be lonely without Charlotte.

She gave him a pained stare as she wrung her hands. "I am not sure marriage is the solution. I have another idea."

"Such as?" He waited for the other boot to drop.

"Your estate is in Scotland?"

"You know it is." A knot formed in his belly as he prepared for her proposal.

She leaned in and whispered, "Have you heard of Handfasting?"

"Handfas--, why not just elope to Gretna Green?"

She placed her hands on her hips. "You know why."

"Yes, yes! No marriage for Charlotte Wold, I'm familiar," he growled. His neck was getting stiff. Why couldn't the woman see reason?

She continued as if he had agreed to her outrageous plan. "Go to your estate. Take care of what requires your attention, and I'll wait here."

"You sound so reasonable." At the moment, he wished he *was* at his estate.

"When my brother, Nigel, arrives, I'll cry off. He will support my decision."

His heart dropped. "Then why handfast at all?"

"That will be our backup plan if this entire matrimony business is unavoidable." She seemed so pleased with herself.

"Can you be so sure? I imagine he will want to see you married once he hears of today's events." He didn't like the idea of her being left to her own devices or perhaps, worse, her slipping away.

"I love Nigel dearly, but he's a simpleton. I can control him, as long as we keep the Fitzwilliams and the Dowlings quiet as well." She increased her stride, pulling away.

"What about the Kendall girls?" He matched her pace. She would not rid herself of him so easily. She might be able to control her brother, but once they were married, and they *would* be married, none of this handfasting business, he refused to be manipulated.

"Trust me. Once he arrives, Amelia and Lord Devonhold will allow me to leave. They will not want the debutantes tarnished by Nigel Philpott."

"Nigel Philpott is your brother!?" Poor Charlotte. The man was a complete idiot. Mr. Phillpot was known for drunken brawls, inebriation, falling asleep in lords' studies, and philandering with matrons of the *ton*.

A flush swept across her cheeks. "He does have a bit of a reputation. I am certain Amelia will want him to be well clear of her family. Come to think of it, Lady Worthington may not want David and Daniel near him either."

"I can't imagine they'd want The Fool--" Myles stopped himself before he revealed anything further.

"The Foolish Rake. Not to worry, Major. I am well aware of his moniker." She gave a half-smile.

He regarded her with solemn wonder. She didn't need him after all. It was ironic that her independence drew him to her, yet it was the very thing keeping them apart. "After you cry off, what will you do?"

"I will stay with my brother. Try and set him on the right path and perhaps help him find a suitable wife."

Myles couldn't help but smile. She was perfectly willing to send other men and women to their fate. Yet, she dared not allow herself to even ponder such an institution. It was maddening. He didn't give up so easily. "And then?"

"I have always loved children, and since I shall have none of my own, I may take a position as a governess."

"Is that why you want to perform an antiquated Scottish ritual rather than marry, because you believe yourself barren?"

"In part, and because I want to be my own person. I don't want to be tied to you."

He didn't bother to reveal the ceremony involved a rope binding them together for a full year. Instead, he asked, "What's wrong with me?"

"Nothing. I didn't mean you specifically, I meant any man. Besides, the thought of an educational position interested me before I rushed into my ill-conceived marriage."

"Why did you? Rush into it?" He needed to delve further into the mysteries surrounding her past if he had any hope of claiming her.

She went rigid. "I preferred to make my own bad choice rather than have my parents make it for me. I can only imagine what kind of aged and rich lord they would have chosen."

Myles frowned. He didn't like to think of her alone, or worse, married to another. Why did her rejection bother him so? He should be relieved since her idea would give them more time together and he had every intention of marrying her in the end. "It sounds as if you have it all planned out."

"I do." Charlotte held her chin up, yet raw hurt glittered in her eyes. "Shall we return and announce our engagement?"

"Yes, we shall."

He told himself her reprieve from wedding shackles was best for distance and perspective. He would use the time to wage war on her heart.

"Handfasting?!" Amelia coughed into her tea as they sat in the sitting room the following day. "You are not serious? You just announced your betrothal last night, and I've made arrangements. Why even now James is --"

Charlotte cut her off. "Oh, but I am." She expected resistance to her idea, so she was prepared. "Besides, it would be in Major Ashton's best interest."

"How so?" Amelia asked.

"If I am barren, then we may go our separate ways and the major is free to find a more suitable bride."

"What about you?"

"I'll be fine. I will return from the adventure, none the worse."

"No, you won't. I don't care how they do things up north. You will not be welcome in polite society after such an adventure, as you call it."

"I don't intend to get married. I intend to seek a post as a governess or a companion."

"No one will want you. No, it is best you and Myles marry right away. James instructed Vicar Barry to issue a license and we will have you married in St. Mark's Chapel before the end of the week."

"No!"

"Charlotte, think of your future," Amelia implored.

"If the *ton* doesn't want me, I will stay with my brother."

"You don't even know where he is."

Leave it to her dear friend to knock down her argument. "If I must, I will join the nunnery, but I will *not* be chattel for some man."

"Myles is not like that."

Charlotte didn't believe he was either, but her instincts had steered her wrong before. Robert had been extremely chivalrous at the start of their courtship, and he loved reading as well as learning French from her, and then somewhere over the years, he lost his way. He became distant, less affectionate, and increasingly cruel. She only wished she knew what happened to change him.

"Charlotte?"

Pulled from her inner tirade, she finally answered, "You don't know what men are like until you are forced to live with them."

"So you want to handfast, to see if you are compatible?" It was the first and only time Amelia had asked about her wishes.

"Yes. I only want to see if he is the man you believe and I hope he is." It was true, the handfasting would allow her to observe what kind of man Myles truly was.

"Charlotte, I do not know what possessed you to marry your first husband, but fate has seen fit to give you another. I guarantee you will not find a better man than Major Ashton. Besides, if you do not suit, you could always get a divorce."

"Divorce!?"

"What do you care? You said you didn't mind what the *ton* thought."

"But a divorce... how dreadful." Charlotte knew she would not be able to go through with it.

"What if you are wrong about marriage?"

She pulled in a deep breath. "I am not."

"What about the man?"

There was a tingling in the pit of her stomach. "Myles?"

"Yes, Myles. In speaking with James, I have learned that Major Ashton is kind and loyal. It is entirely possible you will fall in love with the man and be happy."

Charlotte snorted into her tea. *As if.*

Amelia shrugged. "And if not, you could live separate lives like the rest of the wedded aristocracy."

Two days later, no one was more surprised than Charlotte that she was going through with the marriage. The morning sun filtered through the stained glass windows of St. Mark's Chapel as her feet moved forward toward the groom. She wore a royal blue dress - one of the few new items she owned.

Myles wore a boyish grin from ear to ear and though she should be annoyed, she couldn't help but smile back at him. She prayed Amelia was right about marriage and she had made the correct decision. She had no recourse if this marriage didn't suit her.

When she reached the altar, Myles' warm hands gripped her icy fingers and she looked into his forest-green eyes, letting him anchor her in the moment.

Following the ceremony, the couple was greeted with well wishes which seemed genuine.

The rest of the day went by in a flurry. It seemed no time at all before Charlotte found herself awaiting her groom in his bedchamber.

The door clicked shut behind her.

"Charlotte." His voice tickled along her spine making her warm and tingly.

She turned and drank in the sight of him. "Ashton."

His hair was tousled and slightly damp, curling at the ends. His dark eyes perused her form, causing her to shiver. Perhaps she should have worn something more bridal than her thin nightrail.

"I was wondering if I would see you..." she stammered. Secretly, she wanted his kisses and hopefully, a night of passion.

"Darling, I wouldn't have missed our wedding night for the world." A huskiness lingered in his tone. He made no move, simply stood there, devilishly handsome.

"Oh?"

"Why not let me show you." In the next breath, Ashton was kissing her and pressing her back into the bed.

Myles didn't know how he refrained once he beheld her in her thin nightclothes passing as a nightgown. He lifted his mouth from hers. He stood back to gauge her response. She was flushed but she hadn't resisted his advances. He viewed the outline of her breasts, though he was unable to determine the color of her nipples. He lifted his hand and cupped them.

A rewarding moan escaped her lips.

He kissed a path down her ivory throat. He didn't trust himself to not rip the night rail from her, so he contented himself with suckling a peaked tip through the fabric.

She inhaled sharply but grasped his head tighter to her chest. "Yes, Ashton!"

Myles released the engorged tip and began assaulting the other.

Charlotte gasped and gripped him closer.

When he lifted his head. The color which until now had eluded him was "Rosy pink."

"What?"

"Nothing, my dear," He explored beneath her gown, trailing his fingers along the back of her smooth thigh until he cupped her delectable bottom. "You are perfect." He ran his hand along the curve of her buttocks. "So, bloody perfect."

With each word she widened her thighs, granting access to the red curls between her legs. He almost spent at the sight. He could resist no longer. He ran his hands to her folds, testing her response. "Oh sweetheart, you are drenched."

The look on her face was akin to awe. So, she didn't mind his rough talk. Every aspect of this woman made him feel as though they belonged together. "Shall we help you along?"

Her puss fluttered beneath his fingers, but her body tensed. "I am ready for you."

Myles stared at her. "Are you?"

"Yes. You may take me in whatever manner you please."

Myles stepped back. The mood was broken. He removed his fingers from her and stood in one fluid motion. The thin material dropped covering up newly found treasures.

Charlotte's eyes were squinted shut and her fingertips gripped the sheets as if clinging to a lifeline. They had been moving along nicely, and now she was bracing herself. Against him?

"Charlotte," he said, tentatively.

"Yes, I am ready."

"Open your eyes, sweetheart." He coaxed her as if training a frightened animal.

Her gray eyes stared at him.

"You are *not* ready," he informed her.

"I am," she insisted.

"Fine. *I* am not," he acquiesced.

Her eyes flew to his member. "You appear ready. Am I not...enough?" Her voice sounded hurt, and he wished Robert Wold a long stay in hell.

"Oh God, no. Do not think so. You are bloody gorgeous. I want your first time to be perfect."

She sat up. "Ashton, I am not a virgin." Her gaze traveled upward to his chest. He thought her hands might follow, but they remained at her sides.

He pulled back and met her stare. "I want your first time with me to be unforgettable."

"Does it matter?" she bit her lip.

A hot ache grew in his throat. "It does to me."

"If it pleases you." She slowly feathered her touch up his arms.

He wanted to cheer with approval but spoke in even tones. "I am going to lift you. Wrap your limbs around me."

She complied, winding her arms around his neck and her legs about his flanks. She felt so right, nestled against him. He lifted and rested her on the edge. "You can let go now."

"Do I have to?" She loosened her hold, but her fingers lingered against his chest. "I like touching you."

He rested his forehead against hers. "You may touch me any way you wish."

Her digits fluttered through the hair sprinkled on his chest before she rested them against his nipples. "Are you sensitive?"

"I'll let you find out." He rested a hand against her back, holding her.

She leaned in and explored the tip with her mouth.

A delicious shudder caused his breath to hitch as he waited to see what his siren would do next. She circled her tongue around the brown pebble before sucking it between her lips. Swallowing tightly he tried to remain still under her ministrations. She pulled back and smiled at him. "Was that wrong?"

"God, no! Let me show you." He rolled her nipple between his index finger and thumb. She whimpered. Moving his hand from her breast to her navel, he delved lower to touch her feminine curls. At her gasp, he explored between her damp folds. He dipped a digit into her core and she met his shallow thrust. "Good girl. Ready for another?"

She nodded, her eyes glazing and her head tilting back.

"Hold on to me," he commanded.

The way she gripped him with her muscles, she was getting close to climax. Myles increased the speed and fondled her sensitive button with his thumb. Once he applied pressure to her little bead, Charlotte cried out. He waited for her to come down from her pleasure.

She gazed at him with a relaxed expression.

"Stay with me, love." He lifted her to prevent her from falling back on the bed.

Her movements were languid as she clung to his neck.

"Are you ready for round two?" He looked over her seductively.

"There is more?" Her pink lips parted.

"Watch." He lifted her so he lined up with her on the edge of the bed. His gaze traveled to her face. "So responsive, so beautiful."

Instinctively, her body arched toward him. "Hmm, mmm."

He notched his cock at her opening and slowly pressed forward. She lifted to meet him. "You want me? You want this." The very air around them seemed electrified, but he must be certain she approved before they proceeded.

"Yes." The heels of her feet dug into his flanks.

He pushed until he disappeared inside her. "What do you feel?"

The smoldering flame he saw in her eyes grew as she intently watched their joining. "Full."

He loved her honesty. "Are you uncomfortable?"

"No. I enjoy you inside me," she responded.

Myles pressed her back on the bed. "You are so bloody tight."

Her hands roamed from his neck over his shoulders, and she caressed the length of his back. She planted kisses along his neck.

He captured her mouth beneath his own, darting his tongue into her mouth as his cock plunged into her. Her feet pressed into his buttocks, and he drove into her like a madman. He couldn't get deep enough.

Charlotte cried out beneath him. Her sheath squeezed him tight and he lost himself in her.

Lest he crush her with his weight, he rolled off her, pulling her alongside him. "We must go to Scotland," Myles brushed her hair back and traced her eyebrow with his finger. "I must return home. My neighbor, Laird MacLachlan, is threatening my ward and her mother."

"Of course, go ahead and take care of them."

"I said we. You are coming with me."

She raised on her elbow to look at him. "What? I cannot go with you."

"We are married. We do all things together, Charlotte." The time spent in a carriage would allow him to wear down her defenses.

She seemed ready to argue, but instead remained quiet and settled back against him. He fell asleep to her even breathing.

In the middle of the night he reached for her, but she was gone. Charlotte's departure from his bed indicated she doubted their union. Myles wanted her desperately, for she had etched her name in his heart. His chest hurt at the thought she didn't share these emotions. Regardless, he vowed it would be resolved as they traveled to Scotland.

Chapter Eleven

Morning light filtered in, scattering the darkness. Bird songs floated in from the outside and as she opened an eye, she saw their shadows darting around the room as they took flight.

Charlotte awoke pleasantly sore. She had convinced Ashton she was a bit shy, so they'd made love once more in the dark. It was a relief he'd not been able to see her back and she returned to her room after he had fallen asleep.

They were now lovers, and Charlotte found she didn't mind it at all. A night of Ashton's lovemaking had put Robert to shame. If this was the benefit of being married, then she may settle in nicely. *Until he realizes you cannot bear him heirs.*

Admittedly, Charlotte never minded the more intimate acts with her husband, it was only afterward when Robert was plagued by guilt then he would be hurtful. *"All your red hair, you were made for sin, Charlotte. You would make a better mistress than a wife."* It was all so odd, considering Robert had begun seeing Lisette. Had he been cruel to her as well?

Shaking off her wayward thoughts, she set about getting dressed and then decided against it. She would not travel with Myles to Scotland. She wasn't feeling well. Yes, that sounded reasonable. When Lizzy entered the room, Charlotte handed her a note to give to Myles informing him of her megrim.

Pleased with herself, she crawled back into bed.

Myles fumed as he stood by the front door. The carriage was loaded and the horses were ready but Charlotte's note said she had a headache and advised him to "*go on without her.*"

Did she think he would abandon her? Was that what she wanted? Unlike the rest of the *ton*, Myles had no intention of living apart from his wife. Hell, even his sister lived with her husband and the Marquess and Marchioness of Worthington were as aristocratic as they came.

He took the stairs two at a time and made short work of the hallway. *Damn her!* She was coming to Scotland.

He threw her door open, and it slammed into the wall.

The maid shrieked and dropped the breakfast tray. The china shattered like mortar fire, and tea shot into the air like the Fontaine des Innocents.

"What are you doing?" Charlotte screamed.

"What are YOU doing?" he growled back. "Get dressed."

"I don't feel well."

"You look fine. You can't wallow here all day, just because you've changed your mind." His mouth was dry. He refused to beg.

Lizzy looked up from cleaning the dishes. "Miss Charlotte?"

"Go, Lizzy. I'll be fine with Major Ashton."

Lizzy ran for the door, but not before scowling at Myles before closing it behind her.

"We're married now, so you can use my name." He prayed she didn't hear the desperation in his voice as he paced toward the bed.

She crossed her arms. "I have nothing to say to you."

"Charlotte, why are you fighting this?"

"Because you are being a bastard," she muttered.

He stilled. Perhaps she didn't want him because of his sinful bloodline.

Her face paled. "Oh, Ashton, I didn't mean—"

"Who told you I was baseborn?" Urgent to put distance between them, he stalked to the window.

"Lady Worthington," she huffed.

He wasn't surprised his sister had been the one to broach the subject of his lineage. Joan had always made his life difficult.

"I am not sure how it matters because I did not want marriage."

"Because you have married a bastard?" He leaned against the wall.

"Do not insert words in my mouth. I don't care about your birth status. I simply did not want to be married."

He didn't believe her. "How long have you known about the circumstances of my birth?"

"I do not see how--"

"How long, Charlotte?" He couldn't bear to look at her. He turned to watch the stables.

"Lady Worthington told me the night of the dance, the night we kissed. I assume since you are close to Lord Devonhold you share the same father."

At the sound of her footsteps, he lifted his gaze. "What else did she say?"

She stood by his side. "Nothing. Nor do I care."

He suddenly needed to be away from her. Pushing off the wall, he marched toward the door.

Charlotte grabbed his arm. "Myles, don't leave this unfinished."

He turned toward her.

She stared at him as if she couldn't understand. Perhaps she didn't. Charlotte reached for his hand and he accepted. Sheled him to her bed where she sat and patted the spot next to her. "Tell me about your family."

He reluctantly joined her. "My mother was the late Earl of Devonhold's mistress."

"I assumed as much," she said in a clipped voice.

He rubbed the back of his neck hoping to ease the tension. "Did you know she's still alive?"

She put her hand to her lips. "No."

His gaze was unfocused as he stared toward the window. "She was banished following my birth."

"Myles, I am so sorry." She reached her hand toward him.

He flinched away. "Joan made sure I knew the circumstances of my birth every day. My mother visited on my birthday every year until I left for the army. You see, Joan requested my mother not to be allowed into Devonhold. I only saw her on the road at the gate."

"Through the bars?" Her voice choked.

He wasn't swayed by her emotion. "Yes. Uncle Edgar made certain I knew my mother. Edgar always accompanied me to the gate."

She gasped and reached toward him once again.

This time, he let her fingers grip his forearm. "She was lovely and arrived in a different carriage each time, so I suspect she went through several men over the years."

"Have you seen her since joining the army?" She slithered closer to him so their thighs touched.

"Once. In London. She was working in the theater, and I ran into her having tea in a hotel."

"Did she appear unhappy?" She reached out for his hands.

He accepted and took her hands within his. "No. She was on edge. I suspect she was lying to me and perhaps her new protector was due to arrive. She kept looking toward the exit."

"I'm sorry all this happened to you. I know what it is like to be at odds with parents."

He regarded her with somber curiosity. "Tell me about them."

"I should since you shared so much about your own, but I'm not ready to speak of them yet." She gave him a peck on the cheek. "I just need the day to rest."

"I'm sorry, I must leave to take care of this matter with Laird MacLachlan." He rose and closed the distance to the door. Unable to resist, he looked back at her.

She was tucking a wayward red lock behind her ear. "I will follow as soon as I am able."

"There's no need. Stay with Amelia." A heaviness centered in his chest and dragged his heart down. As the door clicked shut behind him, he wondered if he would ever see his wife again.

Myles slept sparingly on the two-day drive. He woke up from the occasional bump, to relieve himself, and when they stopped to change horses. Sleep eluded him as he could not fall asleep without dreaming of his wife. He wished he had brought Ares. His leg protested being in a stagnant position for so long. Though fully healed, occasionally a nerve would pinch and it was almost as if the wound was fresh all over again. He missed Charlotte and once he sorted this business with Laird McLachlan, he would return to Devonhold and fetch her. He was an idiot for having left things unsettled. His only security was that she belonged to him. She was his wife.

As light entered the carriage, Myles caught his first glimpse of the castle. The roof was gone. One wall had collapsed, and the castle looked more like a tower house, long past its glory.

"Stop!" For some unfathomable reason, he needed to view the destruction of his estate immediately and determine whether it was beyond salvage. Mosswin echoed the crumbling of his heart in his wife's absence. Without Charlotte, he was equally empty and battered.

Myles stepped down, opting to leave his cane in the carriage. His leg needed to walk. Like this crumbling castle, he was still standing, but his insides were gutted, and he faced the world alone. Isolation was probably no less than he deserved for being such a cur.

He closed the distance to the ruins letting his feet roam on his land. Having this piece of ground caused him to increase his gait. His enthusiasm was no comparison to Charlotte in his arms, but nothing would replace her.

Upon closer inspection, there had been a vaulted cellar, and what once must have been a kitchen with a large fireplace hearth. The remnants of two more floors hovered above the hall. At the highest level, a garret projected at the southeast, and two round turrets in the northwest corners. There was no parapet.

Myles imagined this castle could be returned to its former glory. Uncle Edgar had left him significant funds to complete repairs and to care for his mysterious ward. He limped back to the carriage. Mosswin Castle would be a challenge, but nothing insurmountable.

Once settled inside, he tapped the roof with his cane and the carriage resumed its short drive.

Mosswin Cottage stood on high ground above the estate. The house was rather roomy for a cottage, and he suspected this intact home was why the castle remained in ruins. Myles stepped down, rubbed his knee, and grabbed his cane. He hobbled toward the front door.

Before he reached the knocker, the door flung open, and he was greeted by a girl with dark brown hair and bright green eyes wearing a pink dress. "Hello! You must be Major Ashton."

"I am, and who might you be?"

"I am Miss Katherine Fitzwilliam." She smiled and thrust out her hand.

So, this was his ward and uncle's daughter, born to the mistress still residing beneath this intact roof. He accepted her hand, bowing over it, before granting it release.

She didn't wear gloves yet her skin was warm. "Pleasure to meet you, Miss Katherine."

"You can call me Kitty, everyone does," she assured him.

"You may call me Ashton. We are, after all, cousins," he answered.

A voice called from behind Kitty. "Oh, you are a bit closer than cousins."

"Mother!" He could hardly forget the woman who came to Devonhold and then seemed to have disappeared. *What was she doing here?*

"Good afternoon, Myles." His mother, Eleanor Ashton, stood stoically with her fading brown hair pulled back in a severe bun and brown eyes that glowed.

Myles stared, speechless, at the woman who had abandoned him. Her posture was rigid, and she had a look of concern on her face. What right did she have to any emotion? Was she worried he would give her the boot? At this moment, he fancied the idea.

"What are you doing here?" he asked with as chill a tone as he could muster.

"I'd like to speak with you on the matter." She gave Kitty a wary look. "In private."

"You're his mother, too?" Kitty's nose crinkled as she drew her eyebrows together.

Myles stopped mid-stride. His world was spinning a bit. "Wait. Are you the...mistress?"

"Come in." His mother's lips formed a flat line.

He held his ground. "Not until you answer my question."

"Fine." She smoothed her brown skirts before nodding to each of her children.

"Yes, to both of your questions. Now come in."

"This means we are brother and sister!" Kitty squealed.

Myles nearly lost his balance when she threw her arms around his neck with the momentum of a tidal wave. He stabilized his footing and gripped the door frame.

"Katherine!" His mother's voice was sharp.

Kitty released her jubilant hold on him. "Sorry, mother."

"Let us go to the parlor," his mother insisted as he crossed the threshold.

Kitty grabbed his hand. "Follow me."

"Katherine, give us a moment," his mother protested.

Kitty released his hand. She gave his...no, *their* mother a good pout. "This includes me too. Myles is, after all, my brother."

"Katherine, go help Cook assemble a tray in the kitchen and then bring it to the parlor. I am sure your brother is hungry after his long journey." their mother advised.

"Do not start without me. I want to hear everything," Kitty whispered to him before she strode away.

Their mother glided the short distance to the parlor. Once inside, she indicated he should take a seat.

He chose a pastel-colored armchair made of dark wood. The chair was more masculine than the flowers that exploded on the wall, furniture, and in the vases scattered about the room. The smell of roses was pleasant, if not overwhelming.

"You have some explaining to do, and judging from Kitty's enthusiasm, little time to do it," Myles said.

"We will have time," she answered, closing the door with a click, and placing a key in her pocket.

"How long have you been Uncle Edgar's mistress?" He didn't care if he sounded like a bear-garden jaw. His mother owed him some answers.

"I am not Edgar's mistress, I'm his wife."

His muscles went rigid and the room spun. "What? Wife? When did this happen?"

"I am Lady Fitzwilliam. Edgar and I were married long before Katherine was born."

His fingers clenched in the fabric of the chair. "But...why wasn't I notified?"

"You were in residence with Edgar's brother, the earl, whom Edgar could hardly stand, and I've had no correspondence with you since I left." She glanced away, refusing to meet his eyes.

"Why? Was Uncle Edgar distressed that his brother had you first? Was he worried you'd be stolen away?"

"There was no theft, at least not of my person." Her hands balled into fists.

Myles gave her a reproachful look.

The locked door rattled, and Kitty's insistent voice sounded from the hallway. "Mother! Let me in! I have tea and biscuits."

"In a moment," his mother responded with the most serene voice he'd heard since his arrival.

After light footsteps retreated, his mother sank into a chair. "Let me start at the beginning. I have always loved Edgar. I have known him in the biblical sense since before you were born."

Myles threw his hands up. "You were Joan's governess! Where was your sense of propriety?" Being a bastard was bad enough, and he suspected his origins were much worse.

Her hand elevated again. "I was Edgar's mistress long before I was a governess to Lady Worthington."

The fact his mother knew his half-sister had married was not lost on Myles. Had she and his uncle been keeping tabs on his family? Yet, she never revealed where she was, this entire time. He couldn't believe she'd kept this from him.

"Edgar recommended me as governess so we could be together." Her lips tipped upward before relaxing.

"And what? Once you'd arrived, you decided a second son wasn't as good as the first, so you seduced the Earl of Devonhold?" He spat the words.

Her green eyes flashed. "I did not seduce him!"

Myles went silent. He never once considered his conception may have been unwilling. Perhaps his mother couldn't bear the sight of him. "Mother, I..."

She sighed and held her hand up once again. "Myles, let me finish. Then you can berate me and ask your questions."

He nodded, hiding his balled fist in his tailcoat.

"As I said, I accepted a position as a governess to be close to Edgar. Our plan was quite naive. I knew nothing about being a governess. My father was a gambler, and I grew up in the stews of London. By the time

I was twelve, thanks to my father, I had learned how to count cards and read with proficiency."

Myles never suspected his maternal roots were far more uncivilized. He sat dumbfounded. He believed this woman before him a homewrecker of the highest order, and to uncover her lesser origin humbled him. His mouth went dry. Thoughts of self-loathing filled him for believing Joan's detestable stories. He knew life did not grant choices to those less fortunate.

"I knew I would end up earning blunt on my back, but I wanted to have a better life ahead of me. My father died when I was sixteen and I worked in brothels as a servant, disguised as a boy. There I learned foreign languages, including French and Spanish, from working girls. I can read, write, and speak two languages. As you can tell, I have near-perfect diction. These skills convinced the Earl of Devonhold I was a governess."

"Why didn't you become a governess, then?" he asked.

She sighed.

"Sorry, continue."

"You see, my son, I wanted to be a prized courtesan, and I was well aware that elegant lords valued an education. The highest-paid mistresses were educated, often more so than high-born ladies. The path requiring a protector was the most logical conclusion for me. So, I worked in brothels for two years, in disguise of course, before I auctioned off my virginity. I was fortunate the first and only man I have ever slept with was Lord Edgar Fitzwilliam."

Myles was so engrossed in her story he nearly missed it. "Only man?"

"Yes. You see Myles, you are not the bastard son of the Earl of Devonhold. You are the heir of Edgar Fitzwilliam, Laird of Mosswin."

The door to the hall swung open, hitting a side table, and Myles jumped to his feet.

Kitty stood in the hallway, holding a hairpin and wearing an expression he knew very well. Victory. "Ha! I got it!"

His mother stood, resting her hands on her hips. "Dammit, Katherine, what have I told you about discretion and picking locks?"

Chapter Twelve

Charlotte stared out the window, her mood as gray as the weather.

It had been nearly a week since her husband left, and she missed him. Melancholy hung over her like the clouds hanging above the treeline. The day he left she knew no one would replace Major Myles Ashton in the tiny space she granted him in her heart. Did he miss her?

A knock on the door broke through her musings.

"Come in," she replied.

Amelia's blond head peeked around the door. "Are you all right?"

"As well as can be expected." *Though I feel my heart is breaking.*

"Do you want to be alone?" Concern etched her friend's fine features.

"I have many moments in the future, alone." Charlotte hated the bitterness that crept into her voice.

Amelia stomped into the room and she met Charlotte's gaze straight on. "Charlotte Ashton! I have known you for nearly two decades and I've never seen you so forlorn. If your husband means so much to you, put your row with him in the past and move forward."

"Yes... I mean no. Oh, I am not certain." Charlotte wasn't sure if she was prepared to discuss her newly discovered feelings. She cared deeply for Ashton. He was kind and treated her as an equal, ever since they hatched their plan.

"What are you certain of?" Amelia's question was probing.

"I am certain I'll never find another man like Ashton." There, she'd admitted her tendre for her husband.

There was a twinkle in Amelia's blue eyes. "Are you the same girl who arrived and did not want to remarry?"

Of course, Amelia would have to remember her protests. "I am. I still do not believe marriage was the correct solution."

"Then, as you said, does it matter if Ashton is gone?"

Charlotte straightened. "It doesn't. Not one whit."

"Oh, I can see very plainly it does. My dear Charlotte, you are pouting."

"I am not." She lifted her chin and met Amelia's thinly veiled mirth straight on.

"You are. It's been almost a week and Myles hasn't sent for you." Amelia stated. "So, what are you going to do?"

Charlotte grimaced. She was uncertain how to proceed. "I cannot go to him," she said aloud.

"Why not? You are his wife. Eventually, you must travel to Mosswin Castle. I think it's perfectly reasonable to see the home where you will live and the man who has slipped into your heart."

Could she go to him? Could she repair the damage she had done? She imagined herself away from the comfort and safety of Devonhold. Since Lady Worthington had left, there was a quietness. Soon, excitement would fill the air as the London Season approached. The Kendall sisters wanted their Season, and though Charlotte could go with them, she wasn't ready to brave the city quite yet. "I should wait for my brother."

Amelia squeezed Charlotte's hand before speaking with quiet firmness. "Leave Mr. Phillpot to me. Should he send word or heaven forbid, appear on my doorstep, Lord Devonhold will deal with him directly."

"I see there is little reason to argue with your plan," Charlotte conceded. No reason to admit eagerness, and a sense of adventure filled her.

"Wonderful. I will have trunks of new clothing packed for you! Shed the black and rejoin the living, my dear. Of course, James will send you in our best carriage. You can bring along the rest of Myles' things and Ares as well."

"How soon?" Once the decision was clear in her mind, Charlotte could hardly wait to be underway.

"Tomorrow?" Amelia suggested.

"Are you trying to get rid of me?"

"Of course not. I am simply ready to focus on my next match of the Season." Amelia always enjoyed her matchmaking abilities.

"Arabella." Charlotte sensed Arabella was a particular challenge for Amelia with her shy nature.

"Is it so obvious?" Amelia worried her lip. "I merely want her to be happy."

"Like you are?" Charlotte ventured.

"Yes, of course. I knew you'd understand."

"I do." Although currently, Charlotte commiserated more with Arabella. "May I make a suggestion?"

Amelia nodded. "I welcome your opinion, wholeheartedly."

"As someone who didn't make the best choice of husband her first time out, let Arabella have some time. It is best to marry wisely rather than hastily." Charlotte hoped Arabella found love, or at the very least, peace. She suspected it would be hard on the young woman who resembled her outgoing twin in appearance but not personality. The pressure to make a match worthy in its own right might be more than Arabella could bear. Even Charlotte, who was dear friends with Amelia, occasionally felt dull by comparison, and she didn't possess the same good looks.

Amelia nodded. "You are making better choices the second time around."

"I hope so."

"You let her get away with too much," Eleanor scolded.

Myles watched as his younger sibling parried against the oak tree, as they sat in the rose garden taking tea. "I do not see the harm."

"You wouldn't. Katherine has been spoiled since birth. It's our fault -- Edgar's and mine. We experienced such a sense of loss after we were forced to surrender you, so we made up for it by spoiling her."

The oak branch took a beating from his cutlass. "Since Kitty is occupied for a while, I'd like to ask you a few more questions."

His mother frowned and tisked. "You underestimate her attention span."

"Regardless, you haven't addressed how I came to stay with the late earl."

Her brown eyes misted. "Haven't I?"

"If it's too painful..." He tried not to press, but he wanted to understand why his parents abandoned him.

"It is all right. You deserve to know."

He closed his eyes. "Take your time."

His mother drew in a deep breath as if she needed to purge the memory. "When I discovered I was with child, I informed Edgar, and we planned to elope to Gretna Green. Unfortunately, the earl caught wind of our plans and stopped us as we were about to leave. He begged us to stay, said there was no reason we couldn't stay until after you were born. He argued that Mosswin was no place to raise a child." She lay an affectionate hand on one of her roses.

"What happened after I was born?"

His mother glanced toward his sister, yet not watching, a frown on her face. "It's a shame Katherine hadn't been born first. Perhaps we would've been allowed to leave."

"I do not understand."

"The late countess had given birth twice to stillborn boys and lost another one in the crib."

"I had no idea." His lips pressed together in a slight grimace.

"Arthur kept the poor woman pregnant nearly their entire marriage. Because of her 'weakness to produce an heir' he called it, Arthur wanted to name you as his."

"In the event James died?" he asked.

She nodded. "Sometimes I think Margaret must've given her life force to James for him to survive."

"Was it so unbearable you needed to leave? And why didn't you take me with you?" The pleading in his voice was unavoidable.

She reached across the chair to touch his leg. "We did take you with us. Arthur was a bit mad about lineage, so we planned our escape. You were about three months old, and we felt you were strong enough to survive the long and risky journey to Mosswin."

"What happened?"

"Arthur caught us. But Edgar refused to give you up. He argued with Arthur to let us go. He even drew a pistol upon his brother, at which point Arthur agreed to let us leave."

"But not me?"

"That's the thing of it. We thought you were with us until we arrived a good distance away from Devonhold. You were always the perfect babe, and you had been so quiet. We imagined you had slept through our travels. But, when we looked in your basket upon our arrival, we found nothing but root vegetables in bunting."

His driving need to understand prompted him to ask, "How?"

"I had set you down when Edgar drew his pistol. I knew your father would not be able to live with himself if he shot the Earl of Devonhold. I've suspected for some time that young James' nurse, who was bedding Arthur, swapped you while I attempted to diffuse the situation. I now believe the entire argument was a ruse to make the switch."

"Why didn't you try to get me back? Or when James and I came here to hunt, why didn't Father try to keep me?"

"You think we didn't? The minute we noticed you were missing, we went to retrieve you, but Arthur barred us from Devonhold. Eventually, all the *ton* believed you were Arthur's. If Joan had kept her mouth shut, everyone would have believed you were the spare. Since we weren't yet married, Edgar had no legal standing, and what court would give you to a mother who could be painted as a whore?"

Myles nodded. What could he say? He understood the bigotry of the *ton* and their obsession not to soil their pristine lineage.

"After James was named the earl's heir, we again tried to claim you. You may remember Edgar coming to visit when you were about ten?"

Edgar, his real father, gave him his first pony. He took him riding and taught him to hunt and fish. He brought him to see his mother for the first time on the other side of the gate. Myles coughed. "I do."

"Well, he changed his mind when he saw how well you and James got along, and of course, his brother had taken care of you. He was afraid to uproot you from your home."

"There was no home. The old Earl of Devonhold was not affectionate."

"He never had been with anyone."

"He spoiled Joan," Myles protested.

"Lady Worthington, even as a child, was a spoiled brat, from the moment she was born," his mother muttered. "Regardless, we let you remain, and Edgar spoiled you from afar. He made arrangements to have you inherit Mosswin and take care of any future children we had."

Myles recalled the extravagant Christmas and birthday presents sent to him throughout his childhood, some more extravagant than even James and Joan had received. Ares, as well as his expensive commission, had come from his father. "But you never reached out!" Bitterness laced his words. "You let me believe you didn't care." Myles could count the scarce number of times he'd seen his mother at Devonhold.

"It was difficult," her voice hitched. "Your father said I would regret not continuing to visit you."

"Then why did you stop?" The last time he met her at Devonhold was before he went to Eton.

"Katherine was born."

And nothing until he saw her at the inn near London where she claimed to be performing in a play. "At the inn?"

"I had recently returned from London after buying Katherine a new wardrobe. If you had stuck around any longer, you would have met her, as well as your father."

Myles shook his head. "I made a hasty retreat." Fate adjusted his life, and yet here he sat. As if he'd always been the firstborn son of Lord Edgar and Eleanor Fitzwilliam and not a bastard.

"Look!" Kitty approached the table holding a mutilated oak branch.

Myles gaped and then groaned at his sorely abused cutlass.

"See? Spoiled," his mother said before taking a sip of tea.

Chapter Thirteen

By the next day, Myles agreed with his mother. Kitty was indeed spoiled. His sister was used to getting her way with everything.

"I want you to hire a governess for Kitty," Eleanor said over breakfast as Kitty grabbed a confection, drank a sip of tea, and darted away.

"Where is she going?" he asked.

"Probably to go investigate the latest batch of kittens in the barn." Eleanor buttered her toast as if she had given up reigning in his sister.

"Why doesn't she have a governess already?"

"Honestly?" She paused in her buttering.

"Please."

"Well, if they can stomach me, which many cannot, I hire them."

"You and your manners are fine. What do you mean, if they can stomach you?"

"They eschew my lack of breeding... because I was not born into the *ton*. I have found certain household staff desire a family with lineage and prestige."

"I can't imagine the villagers care," Myles scoffed.

"Hah, if I could find a governess in Scotland, I would have. No, I've recruited most of them from England."

"And why did they leave?"

"They disappear after less than a fortnight of dealing with your sister."

"So, she's a bit of a hoyden." At his mother's nod, he asked, "Aren't all girls her age?"

His mother laughed. "If only it were so simple. I think your sister takes a perverse sense of pleasure in tormenting the tutors I hire."

He raised his eyebrows and crossed his arms. "How will I succeed, where you have failed?"

Her mouth turned downward. "I suspect a laird, regardless of his birth, carries more weight than a lady who they consider beneath them."

The memory of Charlotte brought a wry smile to Myles' face. "I may know someone who might be interested in tutoring Kitty."

A slow smile spread over his mother's features. "Oh?"

"My wife."

His mother stabbed her toast. "Wife?"

"Yes."

She gave him a critical squint. "Well, where is this woman?"

Myles scrubbed a hand over his face. "She remained at Devonhold when I departed." He wasn't sure why he felt compelled to reveal his history with Charlotte to his mother, but he spent the next hour relaying everything.

"She wants to be a governess?" Eleanor asked when he was done.

"It is a decision she planned before we were married."

"And you believe she would tutor Katherine?"

"I don't see why not. Unless Amelia and Joan have talked her out of joining me."

"Joan has been a thorn in my side ever since I arrived at Devonhold."

Myles merely nodded.

"I am not certain I wish for this wife of yours near Katherine. Maybe she is one of those religious zealots, given her father and her late husband were both vicars."

He sighed before rubbing his neck. "Do you honestly think I would have married her if she was?"

"Most likely not." Eleanor shrugged, but her eyes made him wonder if she sensed his feelings for his wife.

"Well, as you said, Kitty needs a governess. And I think Charlotte might be willing to take the post."

"For your benefit? Or Katherine's?"

"Both." He sent up a silent prayer hoping she was still at Devonhold.

Charlotte cast her gaze toward the green rolling hills and the white fluffy clouds above. On the last day, it seemed as if they had traveled backward in civilization toward a landscape far more rugged and beautiful.

It was late afternoon, and she was eager to leave the carriage. Though it was the epitome of comfort, it had been over two hours since she last stretched.

"Are you all right, Charlotte?" Miss Arabella Kendall decided at the last minute to accompany Charlotte on her journey to Scotland, and as a traveling companion, she was not much of a conversationalist.

Charlotte suspected Arabella's decision was made to escape her sister's well-laid Season plans. She was happy to support Arabella's subterfuge, and truthfully the girl was an exemplary escort, quietly reading in the corner, and keeping to herself. Unfortunately, Arabella's silence left Charlotte alone with her thoughts for much of the day.

"I admit I am a bit nervous. I took the liberty of traveling when perhaps I should have waited for Ashton to send word." What would Myles think of her traveling to meet him? Was this action too bold? Would he reject her? What if he did? Her stomach churned with the unknown.

"That is the reason I have come with you." Arabella carefully folded a page in her book before snapping it closed and resting it on her lap.

"Oh?" Charlotte raised an eyebrow. "I thought perhaps it was to avoid London and the Season."

Biting her lip, Arabella glanced away. "You saw through my ruse?"

"You forget, I was paraded in front of every eligible bachelor within reason."

"Yes, and now because Amelia has you married off, she's ready to dispense with me."

She allowed memories to surface. "I'm not speaking of Amelia. I had a mother who wished I would marry better."

Arabella set her book on the seat beside her and leaned forward.

Charlotte was no longer trapped by her youthful emotions, and the words rushed forth before she could stop them. "To avoid her choice, I made one of my own, much to my detriment."

"Do you mind if I speak plainly?"

Since Charlotte had never known Arabella, the quieter of the twins, to speak up, she nodded her acquiescence.

"I never cared for the late Reverend Wold." She snapped her mouth shut as she had done to the book earlier.

"May I ask why?" Most people she met hadn't liked Robert, and she was curious as to Arabella's experience with him.

"I suspect the feeling was equivalent to what hens must feel like when the fox has been let into their house."

Charlotte nodded, unable to disagree. Arabella was an apt student of people. Since they had been children, it was as if she had a talent for reading people. She called them feelings; Amelia called them intuition. Perhaps if Charlotte had possessed the feeling or intuition that Arabella held, she would not have married Robert. Then again, her parents' schemes might have seen her married to someone far worse.

The carriage came to an abrupt stop, and Charlotte looked up, startled to find a footman opening the door.

The footman pulled down the stairs, and Charlotte let Arabella exit first. She wasn't quite ready to enter Ashton's domain.

On her exit, the sun chose that moment to burst through the clouds, nearly blinding her with its intensity.

Arabella was already at the door, rapping the brass lion-head knocker.

The footman retrieved Charlotte's valise, and they all stood waiting.

The door flung open, and Arabella moved backward as a lovely young lady with brown hair, green eyes, and an elfish face greeted them exuberantly. "Hello, welcome to Mosswin! My name is Katherine Fitzwilliam. Are you my new governess?"

"No," Arabella said definitively.

The girl fixed Charlotte with a questioning stare.

Charlotte bit her lip. Though she wished to be arriving to teach, she could not be so fortunate. "I do not believe so."

"Wonderful! I would hate to chase you off. You can call me Kitty! Come in." Kitty gestured for them to follow her.

Arabella cringed and gave Charlotte a look as if wondering what kind of madhouse had admitted them. The entrance hall was tranquil with an eggshell pallet while a simple brass lantern hung from above.

Once they crossed the threshold, an older lady met them at the foot of the stairs. "Katherine! Did you answer the door again? Why do we even keep Galahad on?"

"Galahad is resting." Kitty pointed to the corner where an elderly balding man, who could pass for Cobb's brother, sat arms crossed in a chair, sound asleep.

"Do you see these gray hairs?" The older lady pointed to her head of fading brown hair. "These are from this past year and all your antics."

Kitty frowned. "We have guests, Mother."

Kitty's mother stepped forward in greeting. "I am so sorry, ladies. We tend to be a bit less formal here at Mosswin. I am Eleanor Fitzwilliam, Lady Mosswin."

"Hello. I am Miss Arabella Kendall, and this is Mrs. Charlotte Ashton."

"Oh, Myles' wife and our temporary governess! We weren't expecting you for another week or so." Lady Mosswin rushed forward in greeting.

"I am sorry, my lady," Arabella started. "What did you say?"

"Charlotte, my son's wife. Myles wrote to her a few days ago requesting her presence."

Charlotte was confused. Governess? "Where is Major Ashton?"

"He is visiting our tenants." Lady Mosswin stepped away and her eyes narrowed. "If you are not here to educate Katherine, why are you here?" The woman's previous sunny demeanor was replaced by something more overcast.

"Perhaps we should wait until Major Ashton comes back, so he can clear up any misunderstanding," Arabella inserted.

Charlotte was relieved her companion had spoken. She was too stunned to use words in a coherent sentence. She had expected to meet the late Laird Mosswin's mistress and Ashton's ward. Not his mother and sister.

"An excellent idea, Miss Kendall." Young Kitty grabbed Arabella's hand and led her towards a parlor, or perhaps a conservatory, given the number of roses, packed within the room.

"Katherine!" Lady Mosswin's voice rose. To Charlotte, she whispered, "This is why we sent for you. No manners."

Kitty stopped and stared pointedly at Charlotte. "I am no longer speaking to you." She then continued her march to the parlor tugging Arabella along.

Elderly Galahad stirred in the corner. He opened one eye and decided against rising from his nap. He settled back into his chair and went back to sleep.

Lady Mosswin sighed. "I am sorry, Charlotte."

"It is all right." Charlotte was surprised she found her voice. "Honestly, I didn't receive a word from your son. Perhaps I made a hasty decision to travel here."

"Oh?"

"Yes. Your son and I had a misunderstanding."

The woman inspected her fingers. "I am well aware of your feelings toward my son."

Charlotte's cheeks grew warm and stepped backward. "I...am sorry."

"You misunderstand me. I care not a whit if you are my son's employee, lover, or wife." Her words belied a veiled lace of censure.

"You... You are... not?"

"No. My concern is with you parading my son around by his heartstrings."

"Lady Mosswin, you are mistaken. Your son bears no feeling for me." How could he after she'd all but abandoned him?

The woman peered her over and shook her head. "Humph. You do not know my son at all."

Charlotte felt her eyes watering and pressed her fingers into her gown to keep from wiping them.

"Mother!" Ashton's voice sounded behind her.

Charlotte turned to find Ashton with hands on his hips. His eyes were flinty and his face red. She could not ascertain if his anger was directed at her or his mother. Regardless, it was good to see him in his white linen shirt and fitted leather riding breeches. He held a dark coat in his hands. Oh, she had missed the sight of him!

"Myles. Well, I'd best see if our other guest has been attended to." Lady Mosswin didn't even bristle. The woman had already washed her hands of Charlotte.

Lady Mosswin stepped lightly over and nudged the sleeping Galahad.

The servant rubbed his eyes and stretched before looking up. "My lady?"

"Bring some tea and biscuits to the parlor." Lady Mosswin left the room, leaving Charlotte's mind racing as to what would happen next and how to keep from further embarrassment.

The servant moved at a snail's pace to the back of the house and his mother shut the door with a loud click to the parlor. Myles could barely contain himself when he turned to Charlotte. "You are here." Though he hoped she would come, he was worried that, left to her own devices, she would further avoid him.

"My brother hasn't returned, and I decided to come here. You sent for me?" Charlotte pursed her full lips. He fought the temptation to draw her into his arms.

"I did. Walk with me?" He offered her his elbow.

She paused before she accepted, and he steered her outside. He told her of the letter he sent requesting help with Kitty. "You do not have to be her governess."

"I would like to help. I'm sorry I missed your missive. Instructing your sister will give me something to do."

"I suspect she will give you a bit of a fight," Myles confessed. "She has chased off quite a few governesses."

"Well, as your wife, I cannot be chased away. How is it that your mother and sister came to be here?"

"It turns out my mother is the wife of the late Edgar Fitzgerald, who was also my father." At her puzzlement, he gave her a brief account of his history. "I am the legitimate heir of Mosswin."

"Congratulations. So, you only requested my presence to help with your sister." Her head lowered and her shoulders slumped.

"No! Tutoring Kitty was only a ruse. I hoped once you arrived, you would stay."

She lifted her gaze and met his eyes. "So, if I refuse, you will send me elsewhere?"

"Of course not. I want you at my side."

Charlotte shook her head. "That is a relief. I--" She stopped.

Myles turned back to see what had her so entranced. They had walked to the ruins. "This is Mosswin Castle. What do you think?"

"It's..."

He supplied words so he wouldn't have to hear them from her lips. "Hideous, decrepit, empty..."

"Beautiful." Awe filled her voice.

Myles stepped back, allowing her to pass. Charlotte's eyes widened as she strode in earnest to the top of the hill, and he rushed to keep pace with her. "You think so?"

"Do you plan to rebuild it?"

"Yes. My father left me substantial funds, so if I can make the necessary repairs."

"It will look very grand once you do."

Charlotte was able to see potential in everything except herself. She had no idea how beautiful she was to him, or perhaps, to anyone else. His heart thumped faster in her presence. There was no longer any doubt: this woman was meant to be his wife.

Chapter Fourteen

Charlotte sighed.

Yet again, Kitty was nowhere to be found. The girl was tenacious in evading her lessons. Kitty had no desire to learn, which was a pity, as she was extremely bright. Fortunately, Charlotte had pursued the miscreant to all her haunts in the last few days, so she knew where to look for her. She donned a bonnet as she descended the staircase to search for her wayward student. When she reached the landing the Matriarch of Mosswin Castle halted her.

"Charlotte. A word, please." Lady Mosswin crooked her finger much the way her mother used to.

Wishing to avoid whatever confrontation lay before her did no good. This was Myles's mother, so Charlotte followed her into the parlor. This place might as well have been a throne room from Medieval times. Once the lady sat in her chair, she ruled all she surveyed and at this moment, the kingdom included her. Charlotte refused to let the woman rattle her. "Yes, Lady Mosswin?"

The woman gestured to a nearby settee. "Have a seat."

Charlotte sat as instructed and prepared herself for a lecture.

Once seated, the question came. "What are your intentions?"

"As to what, my lady?" Her stomach was tight and hard, the question all too familiar. *Charlotte, what are your intentions and why do you insist on socializing with Doctor Kendall's offspring? They are beneath you.*

"As to my family—my daughter and my son." Lady Mosswin crossed her arms.

"Currently, I am in the process of finding Kitty."

The older woman shivered. "Katherine."

"I am looking for her, so we may begin our lessons."

"Lessons in?"

"Seeing as Katherine is a bright girl, I was looking to encourage her outgoing nature with some horseback riding to free her of energy before we begin. Then, as she already reads and writes with proficiency, I thought perhaps we could explore another language."

Lady Mosswin leaned forward. "Why only one?"

"I am sorry, my lady, I only speak French. However, I understand from Major Ashton you speak three languages."

"I do."

"Is French one of them?"

"It is."

"Would you be amenable to joining us in the French lesson, then perhaps you and Ki-Katherine could work together on mastering additional languages?"

"Exposing Katherine beyond the French standard seems wise. What do you plan to do about her manners?" She pressed her lips together.

"I suspect your daughter might be more easily rendered with the help of Miss Kendall."

"How so?"

"Have you noticed Katherine has impeccable table manners at dinner when Arabella is present? However, those manners seem to slip away when Miss Kendall is not absent at breakfast?"

The matriarch merely nodded.

"Katherine knows how to behave; she simply chooses not to. You may be certain when you take her to London for a Season, she will be up to snuff." Though it grated on her to prepare Kitty like a lamb to the slaughter, she suspected it was what all mamas wanted to hear.

The matriarch crossed her arms. "Well, you seem to have my daughter well in hand. What do you plan for Myles?"

Charlotte bristled. "Lady Mosswin, with all due respect, you do not have a say in what goes on between your son and me."

"My dear Charlotte, my son is in love with you, and you are his wife. Personally, I do not think you are good enough for him, but—"

"I am not."

"Exactly. Wait... what?"

Charlotte smiled inwardly. A moment ago, the woman was in high dudgeon, but this took the wind out of her sails.

"I agree with you. I am *not* good enough for your son. He deserves better than the likes of me. He deserves someone pure of soul. I am not innocent or worthy." Had she not been seated, her knees would have buckled. She wanted to tell the woman more but Myles deserved the truth first.

Lady Mosswin's brow furrowed. "You care for my son."

"I do." Pressing her hand to her chest, she nodded at the sincerity of her statement. "Lady Mosswin, let me make this abundantly clear. I love Major Ashton, but what lies between us is not your concern. I will continue to help with Kitty because Myles asked me to. Not because you demand it. Now if you'll excuse me, I must find your daughter."

Charlotte rose from her seat and strode from the room, impatient to find the youngest of the infuriating Fitzwilliams.

Charlotte eventually found Kitty by the stream, pole in hand, trying to catch a brown trout. "Kitty!"

The girl turned and dropped her pole, lifted her skirts, and prepared to run.

"Do not test me! I will chase you down." Charlotte halted as she heard her own mother's voice.

Kitty ignored the command and ran anyway.

So be it. Charlotte lifted her skirts and gave chase.

The girl was fast, but once she realized Charlotte was in pursuit, she became reckless. Kitty glanced over her shoulder with disastrous results: she collided with a fallen tree and released a piercing cry.

Charlotte slowed, stopping directly in front of her charge. "Are you all right?"

Kitty rubbed her ankle. "No! I think it's broken. This is all your fault."

Charlotte placed her hands on her hips. "I didn't skip out on lessons and run away when told not to."

Kitty crossed her arms over her chest. "If you weren't here, I wouldn't have to run. I could stay--"

"At Mosswin forever?" Charlotte tentatively finished for her.

"Well, not forever." Kitty wrinkled her brow, reminding her of Ashton, and more recently, Lady Mosswin.

"Oh? What is your awe-inspiring plan, then?"

"I am going on a grand tour like young men do! Why shouldn't young ladies be allowed the freedom to travel?"

"Why indeed," Charlotte acknowledged.

"Why are you agreeing with me?" Kitty's eyes narrowed on her.

"Why not? I have your best interests at heart," Charlotte answered truthfully.

Kitty scoffed. "You only want to see me married, like Mother and Myles."

"Is that what they've said?" Charlotte had a difficult time imagining Myles wanting his sister rushed into a marriage.

"Well, no."

"Then where did you get the idea?"

"Abigail Brigman went for her Season last year and was married off right away. No one has seen her since." Kitty sniffed, but Charlotte could tell it was pure drama. The girl's voice lacked the pitch of anguish.

"Miss Brigman was your friend?"

Kitty nodded.

"And your mother decided you should have a Season as well?"

When Kitty didn't respond, Charlotte asked, "Have you told your mother you do not wish to marry?"

Kitty laughed bitterly. "What is the point?"

"She might surprise you."

"You can't be sure. Laird MacLachlan has threatened to steal me if my mother doesn't allow me to marry him."

Charlotte was so stunned at the brutality of theft upon Kitty that she spoke without thought. "Myles would not let that happen."

"How can you be certain?"

"Your brother would not let someone take you." She was as certain of this as her next breath.

"You cannot know."

"Oh, but I can. You see Kitty, I had a matchmaking mother who wanted to marry me off to better *her* circumstances. Something tells me your mother is not like mine, or other mothers of the *ton*. If she were, she'd have employed a stern governess who beat you."

Kitty's sniffles ceased.

"So, who is going on this glorious adventure with you, and where are you going?" Charlotte asked.

Kitty's mouth gaped like a brown trout out of water, gasping for air. "I...uh..."

As she suspected, Kitty hadn't planned beyond the moment. Charlotte fired her next questions in rapid succession. "Who will you travel with? How will you speak to the locals? What sites will you visit? Will you travel by land or water? How will you exchange funds?"

"I hadn't thought much about it," Kitty confessed as she rubbed her ankle.

"Clearly. Would you like to?" Charlotte wondered if perhaps her injury was faked as well or at the very least not serious since the girl now seemed focused on their conversation.

"How?" There was the Fitzwilliam furrowed brow again.

"Well, to start, you could spend time with your mother. She speaks three languages. She'll be joining us for your French lessons. And we could look at some of the maps in the library and learn about places you'd like to visit."

"Like Greece?"

"Greece and any country or city to tickle your fancy. We could then tailor lessons around your interest in travel and adventure. Learn bits of the language, customs, dress, and so forth." As Charlotte spoke, a plan formed in her mind. If she could help Kitty, perhaps she could help other young ladies find their adventures. The idea held merit.

Rising, Kitty stepped forward and screamed in pain. Giant tears fell from her green eyes.

Charlotte leaned over and examined her ankle, which had doubled in size and was turning red; the injury was real. "I fear your ankle may be broken. Can you wait here while I go get help?"

Kitty nodded silently, seating herself on the oak log that had felled her. It was a shame that her student needed to be lame before seeing the benefit of an education. Charlotte made haste in the direction of the house.

Chapter Fifteen

Myles came upon his wife as she strode toward him. She didn't yet see him with her bonnet blocking her view. She was watching the ground. "Charlotte!"

She waved at him and turned away, gesturing for him to follow.

He chased after her until she turned the bend, and he lost sight of her. He increased his pace and found Kitty sitting on a fallen oak. Charlotte was at her feet.

"What happened?"

Charlotte said without looking up, "Kitty has hurt her ankle. It may be broken."

Myles rushed to his sister's side. "Can you bear weight on it?"

Kitty shook her head.

Myles lifted his sister in his arms and proceeded back to the house. "How did you fall?"

Charlotte rested her hand on his arm. His skin tingled where her fingers gripped him. "Not now, Ashton."

They made their way in silence back to the house.

Galahad greeted them at the door. "Sir?"

"Have someone fetch the local doctor. Kitty has injured her foot."

Arabella Kendall glided from the parlor, followed by his mother.

"Why are you carrying Katherine?" Concern etched his mother's face.

"Kitty injured her leg." Myles climbed the stairs, the rustle of skirts following in his wake. He strode the length of the hall to her room on the far end. Once inside, he deposited his sister gently on the bed.

Miss Kendall spoke first. "If you allow us, sir, we will help Katherine disrobe."

"Yes, yes," his mother chimed in.

He and Charlotte exited the room. Once the door closed, words tore from his mouth. "What on earth was she doing? Climbing a tree? Jumping rocks in the stream?"

Charlotte gave him a look that would no doubt shrivel the cockles of a lesser man. Her stare simply made him want to take her into his arms. "Nothing quite so dramatic. She tripped and fell."

Myles' heart sank. "Did you have to chase her down?" Though he knew the answer, he wanted confirmation before he locked his sister in a bloody tower.

"What morning have I not had to track down Kitty?"

"I'll speak with her." He paced across the floorboards, eager to take action.

"That is not necessary." Charlotte's face held a ghost of a smile.

The lively twinkle in her gray eyes only incensed him more. He threw his hands up. "Not necessary! Do you want me to wait until she breaks her bloody neck?"

"No." Her face was a picture of serene calm. "While your sister was receptive, I seized the opportunity to speak with her."

Her demeanor made him want to punch something. He sorely wished he was in his mother's rose-roomed parlor. "Receptive? Do you mean incapacitated?"

"As I said, *receptive*. At the moment, vulnerability tends to alter Kitty's perspective." The look on her face said she was losing her patience. Good, let her rail at him. He was ready. She said nothing.

After a few moments of silence, he relaxed and felt like an ass. It was his turn to smile. "I am sorry. Continue."

"Kitty and I have arranged a lesson plan around her goals and what she finds important."

"You are letting a sixteen-year-old girl decide her education." He was dubious at best.

"Yes, but it's not as roughshod as you think. She wants to travel."

"Travel? But she's little more than a child."

"She won't be a child forever. What would you have become of her, Ashton? Do you mean to marry her off to better your social standing or avoid an altercation with the neighboring laird? Perhaps keep her locked in this cottage?"

He frowned at her.

"I know, let's build a tower, and then she can remain safe and locked up." Charlotte's voice was thick with sarcasm.

"You know I do not want any of those things." Though he renounced her, the idea of tucking his sister safely away held appeal.

"Then let Kitty have some say in her future! Her compliance will be the best way to encourage her education. She's already agreed to French lessons, and she wants to learn more about geography and history."

Myles tilted his head and scratched his chin.

"Perhaps simply the French lessons." Charlotte shuffled her kid-slippers which were now grass-stained thanks to his sister's antics.

Since she arrived, there had been nothing but trouble with Kitty and altercations with his mother.

"How are you doing for a wardrobe?" he blurted.

"I am fine," she bristled.

He sensed now was not the time to push her, so he asked again after Kitty. "What about her boundless energy?"

"I thought to work with her on horsemanship, and perhaps you could teach her pistols and pugilism."

"Pugilism? Are you daft?"

"What is wrong if she grasps how to fight?"

"Just because I scoffed at your tower idea doesn't mean I think Kitty-" he paused in his tirade. To smile. "Though if any woman could master pugilism, it would be her. I do not think my sister is ready for fighting. Next, you'll recommend she attend gaming hells."

"Do not be obtuse. I was thinking more for her safety, should she travel or even if she does not." Her mouth drew into a straight line, and she bit her lip.

"She won't need those things. I will protect her."

"You won't always be there, Myles. She should be able to protect herself in the event someone else cannot." Charlotte was still and any warmth she'd had was gone.

The stricken look on her face forced his question. "Who hurt you?"

"Me? No one has hurt me." She stepped back. "I need to go over tomorrow's lesson plan for Kitty."

Charlotte darted from the room, escaping further questioning. He would get to the bottom of this later.

Unfortunately, his wife did not arrive at dinner or come to his room in the evening. She must be well and truly mad at him, and there was little he could do. He tossed and turned, twisting the bedding around his limbs. What had he done? Well, he was finished wondering. If she wouldn't come to him, he would go to her.

Myles reached for the adjoining door. He turned the doorknob and was relieved to find it unlocked.

Charlotte was sound asleep.

He gripped the fabric of his dressing gown and debated for a half-second turning around. No, they needed to talk. He needed reassurance that she was well. More importantly, assurances that things were settled between them.

He tiptoed to the bed until he loomed over her. She was so peaceful, and he didn't want to wake her with his barrage of questions. While she had married him, they disagreed on the very nature of their relationship. She refused to spend the night in his bed and acted more like an employee than his wife. He wanted the air cleared so they might proceed. Or she could leave him.

Charlotte shifted in her sleep. Had she heard him thinking? Her luminous eyes turned on him. "Ashton?"

"Can you see me, then?"

"Of course not," she chuckled. "I simply can't imagine a more imposing figure arriving at my room after dark."

"Imposing?"

"You are like a gargoyle guarding Westminster Abbey," she replied, sitting up.

"As imposing as all that." He rather liked the idea of watching over her and protecting her from evil. Myles knew better than to voice his opinion aloud. She wouldn't appreciate his need to shield her.

"Join me?" Shadows moved below him as she folded back the coverlet.

He slid in easily beside her. Darkness hid her curves from him, but he knew her body well enough. He reached and held her about the waist. She gasped at his touch. He was surprised she was nude. His Charlotte always arrived at his room in one of her button-up nightgowns and if she stayed, they hid her lovely form from his perusal at daybreak. Perhaps in the safety of her room, she was less prim.

Once she rested against the length of his body, he began kissing her. His lips brushed across her collarbone and between her breasts. With a destination in mind, he continued his trail to her golden-red-covered mound. He could hardly wait to plunge his tongue into her, to taste all she was. He stopped at her navel, perhaps waiting for her to stop him with sudden sensibilities.

She did not. If anything her eagerness was expressed as she applied pressure to the top of his head and tilted her hips upward.

Unwilling to miss this opportunity, he ventured further south. Her delicate musk scent wafted to his nose and his mouth pressed a kiss atop her mound. He found her tiny bead of pleasure before his fingers traced lower and parted her and darted his tongue to explore the inside of her.

"Oh, Myles!" Charlotte used his birth name whenever she was caught off-guard. Much as he enjoyed his name upon her lips, he wished she was comfortable to always use it.

He continued his intimate touch until she was panting heavily.

"More," she begged.

"Of?" He lifted his head. Myles wanted her to speak her mind.

"Fingers... something to fill me." A slight tremor filled her voice.

He feathered his first two fingers along her folds, teasing her.

She pressed into his touch, drawing them inside. "Oh, yes!"

Bringing his thumb to her pearl, he strummed the sensitive bud with the pad. Her hips lifted off the bed, he cradled her, and she shuddered in climax against him. As she was coming down, he rose and plunged into her wet, gripping heat. He buried himself deep inside her. How could he stay away? She was everything to him and so much more.

Her hands clutched his shoulders, and he bent to capture her soft lips.

"I love...love...this," she whispered, pulling him closer to her.

Myles reached his climax and abandoned himself to pleasure. He didn't even think to leave, and he had no intention of ever parting from her bed.

He felt her smile when she kissed him.

He rolled off her and dragged her to his side. He stared into the darkness. Once he heard Charlotte's steady breathing of sleep, his own eyes closed.

"Dear Lord, what happened to your back?" Ashton's words were the first indicator she'd overslept and a reminder she'd forgotten to put a nightgown back on.

"It's in the past." She hoped Myles would let it go.

"Did your sorry excuse for a husband do this?"

So much for letting it go. "I do not want to talk about it."

"Charlotte, if your husband didn't do this, who must I call out?" His voice was raised but then lowered as if he struggled to bridle it.

She rose from the bed to her wardrobe and threw on a robe, though it was too late to hide the ugliness of her past. She turned to face him. "Do not call anyone out. A duel will only further embarrass me."

"Who?" He was beginning to sound like an angry owl.

"Promise me." Her muscles tightened as she struggled to maintain an even tone.

"I can't—"

"Ashton, it doesn't matter. Let it go." Biting her lip she looked away. She couldn't bear it if anything happened to him pursuing justice for her.

"Against my better judgment, I will not call anyone out," he said through gritted teeth.

She took hesitant steps back to the bed. "My father."

His fists clenched the sheets. "That bastard."

She stared down at him. "You promised." She found his anger on her behalf satisfying, even though she didn't want him to act on it.

"I am sorry. Continue."

"As you know, my parents wanted my brother and I to elevate their place in this world."

"Your brother too?"

She sat at the foot of the bed, not ready to touch him. "I assume so, though I have no idea what their intentions were. He speaks more languages than I do. Perhaps he suffered worse because our mother held no qualms about beating him. I remember when I met the man who would become my husband, Robert. Nigel was with me, and he spotted my fascination with the man immediately. 'Leave home,' he said. He told me Robert was old enough to keep Father and Mother at bay, but he worried about me. We plotted my escape together, and I eloped with Robert."

"From the boiling pot into the fire."

There was no avoiding the conversation ahead, and it was past time to confess. "Robert was wonderful at first, but he acted as if he deserved more from life. More from *me*. I think he hoped I would elevate *his* station." It seemed as if everyone had wanted something from her to better their life, but not this wonderful man in front of her. He simply wanted her as if she was enough.

"Didn't you?"

"I never had the opportunity. Before I could use a connection such as Amelia, he had already begun an affair with Lisette. Robert was killed in the brothel where Lisette worked. Shot in the heart." Now it was out, she could let him judge her husband and her. If he no longer cared for her, then she was better off. She pulled her knees to her chest. "Perhaps I deluded myself to relieve my conscience."

Myles moved closer and gathered her in his arms. "You didn't know of his activities, so why should you have any guilt?"

Charlotte struggled to accept his touch. She needed to confess her fear before they left the room. "I taught Robert French, which is how he connected with Lisette. Trust has not come easy, and given my abusive father, philandering husband, and wayward brother, I have no good role models. I couldn't help wondering if there was something wrong with me?"

He grasped her chin, turning her face toward him. "What they did had nothing to do with you."

Overwhelmed Charlotte burst into tears. "I should never have married Robert, no matter what my father did," she sobbed. It was too much. No man had ever given her such kindness. It was no wonder she loved him, and she did love him. There was no denying it.

His hands wandered gently over her back, and her tears subsided. "Is this why you wanted me to teach Kitty to fight?"

"Yes," she hiccupped. Though she felt relief for having confided in him, she should have revealed her mistrust sooner.

"I'll start today."

"Thank you." She was relieved Kitty wouldn't have to be a member of the weaker sex despite being the fairer one. "If that is all, I'd like to get started with my day." She rose from the bed uncaring how much damage he witnessed.

Ashton inhaled sharply behind her. "Charlotte."

She turned waiting for something, but unsure what he would say.

"Thank you for telling me."

Nodding, she hastily retreated to her dressing room and readied herself for the day.

Charlotte drew a deep breath before exiting into the hall, where Kitty, now with a bandaged foot and a cane, greeted her cheerfully, "Good morning! What am I to learn today?"

"How about if we discuss plans for your grand tour?"

"Glorious adventure," Kitty corrected with a smile that could not be contained. At Charlotte's puzzled look, Kitty clarified," It sounds so much better. Does it not?"

Charlotte couldn't help but smile. "I suppose it does."

"Besides, I like to think I deserve a bit of an adventure."

"I do too." Charlotte couldn't disagree with the girl's logic.

They reached the breakfast room to find Lady Mosswin already seated, along with Arabella.

Kitty limped, rather gracefully, to the sideboard selecting items before hobbling over and seating herself at the table. "Galahad?"

The butler uncrossed his arms, unceremoniously stretched, and opened an eye as if wondering who would disturb his morning nap.

Kitty waved her hands.

Galahad squinted at the young Miss Fitzwilliam, unenthused.

"Would you bring tea to the table?"

Galahad sighed. "Yes, miss." He finally rose and shuffled off to do his duty.

Charlotte shook her head. Having not grown up with servants, she wasn't familiar with such insubordination. Focused on the butler's lethargy, she nearly missed Lady Mosswin's question. "Well Charlotte, what have you promised Katherine that finally convinced her to join us for breakfast?"

The woman was going to discover what she'd done anyway so might as well tell her now. Charlotte shot Kitty an encouraging smile, but the girl was staring at her plate as if the coddled eggs were fascinating fare.

Frowning, she answered the matriarch in her charge's stead. "I promised her the world."

Kitty looked up from her plate with an eager grin and the same laughing eyes seen many times on her brother. A look she hoped to see again in the future on both siblings.

Arabella began coughing, but Lady Mosswin was made of sterner stuff.

"Did you? Pray tell, how will you manage such a feat?" Lady Mosswin leaned forward ever so slightly in her chair.

Charlotte launched into her campaign because truthfully, she would need the lady's support. "Miss Fitzwilliam wants to go on a grand tour."

"*Glorious adventure,*" Kitty said.

"My apologies. Yes, a glorious adventure."

Lady Mosswin raised an eyebrow, another feature Myles possessed. These subtle characteristics made his mother less forbidding.

"And for any lady to travel, it would be beneficial for her to speak the language, learn about the country, and perhaps understand its culture," Charlotte said.

"Learning those subjects is all well and good, but Katherine only speaks one language, and not proficiently. You speak only French, so am I expected to hire more tutors?" She glanced around the room, looking before shaking her head.

Charlotte drew a deep breath and waved aside her hesitation. "I envisioned you could tutor her in language, my lady, since I understand you speak three."

"Truly, Mama?"

"Yes." Lady Mosswin replied curtly.

"Which ones?" Kitty asked.

"French, Spanish, and Italian. I suppose I can spare some time if she's willing to learn. What about her safety? She can't travel the continent alone."

"I believe this is where I will be involved in Kitty's lessons." Ashton entered the breakfast room.

"You?" Lady Mosswin sighed heavily and rolled her eyes. "You don't have the time."

"I will make time for Kitty. Charlotte has shown me a woman's safety is paramount and she should be able to defend herself in close quarters. Wouldn't you agree, Mother?"

Put on the spot, Lady Mosswin contemplated her children and decided she was outnumbered. "I suppose. So will you go on this glorious... adventure with your sister, Myles?"

Ashton had gathered his plate and was now seated. His gaze found Charlotte and he lazily appraised her. "I rather thought *you* would. After all, you know three languages. Have you no desire to speak these native tongues in their land?"

"Well, not the French." Lady Mosswin blanched. "Perhaps Tuscany."

"Myles, I do *not* need Mama going with me. Her presence will encumber the adventure," Kitty tapped her foot beneath the table and fidgeted with her silverware.

"There is nothing wrong with traveling with one's mother."

"So, you'll join us?" Kitty asked.

"I will not. I will be busy being..."

"Lairdly," Charlotte supplied as she smiled at the family's antics.

"Yes, thank you. I will be busy being lairdly... or perhaps lairding?"

"I believe lairding would be the correct term," Arabella said.

"Thank you, Miss Kendall," Myles' eyes danced as he responded.

"If you would not mind a companion, I would happily go on this glorious adventure with you." Arabella tilted her head to the side.

"Anything to avoid marriage?" Charlotte whispered to her.

Arabella nodded and then spoke to those gathered. "I could help Kitty select a wardrobe, with Lady Mosswin's oversight, of course."

The matriarch nodded. "Of course. I've noticed you've impeccable manners, dear. Perhaps we could help Katherine along with some finishing touches."

The table began to buzz like bees as the group decided where to visit first, what time of year to travel, and what to pack.

Ashton was the first to rise. "I see no reason not to teach Kitty defense straightaway."

The girl pouted. "Myles, I have a sprained ankle. I can't learn anything."

"Not so. I'll show you how to incapacitate a villain using your cane," Ashton assured her. "Meet me in the garden."

Kitty beamed. She rose and slowly followed her brother out.

"I'd best pen a letter to my sister and let her know I will be delayed. Please excuse me." Arabella exited the breakfast room as well.

"Well Charlotte, it seems as if you've gotten me to teach Katherine two foreign languages, Miss Kendall to handle my daughter's finishing, and my son to teach her combat. We may no longer require you as a governess." Eleanor sipped her tea.

"My goal was to ensure Kitty's education, Lady Mosswin, and with proper motivation, she will learn eagerly."

"Whatever will you do now?"

Charlotte couldn't resist her next words. "Perhaps, as your son's wife, I will teach him a few things."

Lady Mosswin smiled and raised her cup. "Well played, my dear. Well played."

Chapter Sixteen

Over the following week, Kitty recovered and rapidly pursued *Canne de combat*. Myles was impressed with her martial and social progress. The more he considered his sister and mother traveling the continent, the more he liked the idea of Kitty having a glorious adventure. Why shouldn't she? With his mother on the trip, he needn't worry about her getting into trouble— and they'd be out of his hair. What a shame he hadn't found Charlotte sooner! If only others like the Kendall girls could benefit from a school with a curriculum geared toward bold and adventurous young ladies.

When he threw his next blow, Kitty parried as instructed.

"Laird?" The door opened behind him, and the footman appeared.

Distracted, Myles looked up, Kitty's cane landed smartly on the back of his calf. "Yes," he grunted. Another blow landed - this time on his back. "Kitty, stop!"

At his command, his sister dutifully stepped back, her smile as innocent as a child in church.

"Yes, Rogers?"

"There is a guest here for Mrs. Wold."

"Who?"

"I do not know. He refused to give his name. Demanded to see Mrs. Robert Wold."

"He did? Hmm." Though Myles trusted Charlotte implicitly, he was curious about who would have ventured to the wilds of Scotland. "Have one of the maids fetch Charlotte."

"Your pardon, m'Laird, but, Lady Mosswin has taken the other ladies into the village for some shopping."

"Very well. Show the gentleman to the study."

"As you wish." The servant rushed toward the steps to the house.

"Shall I go with you, Myles?" Kitty asked from his back.

He turned to face her. "I am sure I can handle it. However, since Mother and your tutors have abandoned their charge, you may join me."

She smiled wide. "Excellent! I'll bring my cane."

They marched to the study, and when the servant opened the door, they found Nigel Philpott gazing out the window.

Myles carved his hands through his hair, staring at Nigel through the open door, and relief washed over him. Nigel's presence indicated the man would acknowledge the marriage, and Myles felt he'd likely be driven to violence if he faced Reverend Philpott directly. He would have words with Charlotte's brother away from her ears.

Nigel stood nearly as tall as Myles but had a bit of a paunch. His hair color was shades lighter than Charlotte's, tied back in a jaunty queue and fashioned with a velvet ribbon. The man was a dandy, bedecked in buff pantaloons and a bright red jacket that echoed the colors of the many and diverse varieties of roses with which his mother had ornamented the room. When Nigel turned his head to look at them, the bloom on his cheekbones matched the crimson hue of the cabbage roses on the still life mounted on the wall behind him.

Myles cleared his throat. "Mr. Philpott."

Nigel spun on his heels. "Do not Mr. Philpott me! Where have you hidden my sister?" he demanded.

"She isn't here."

"Do not lie to me! I went to Devonhold and was told she had traveled across the border to Scotland, of all places." Philpott threw up his hands.

"She is not here *at the moment*. Charlotte went to the village with my mother and Miss Kendall."

Mr. Philpott paused. "With your mother?"

"Yes. Is her absence a problem?"

"Lord Devonhold and your solicitor informed me a mistress was in residence, along with a bastard daughter—Ow!"

Myles bit back his laughter when Kitty struck Philpott across the shoulders with her cane. But he intervened when she readied to strike the man again.

"Why did you hit me, you chit!" Philpott turned toward Kitty. He raised his hand to fend off future blows, yet made no motion to retaliate against her.

"I am not a bastard, and my—our!—mother is a lady, married to our father. Not that the likes of you would bother with the facts of the matter." Kitty was fuming.

Philpott considered Kitty for a moment, still wary of the cane, and then nodded his apology. "I am sorry, miss. I was misinformed."

Kitty lowered her cane.

Myles allowed his smile to escape briefly. Kitty's innocent strength reminded him of Charlotte's back and how his wife had suffered at the hands of her family. Then his smile faded. "Hit him again, Kitty."

His sister happily obliged.

"Bloody hell! What was that for?" Phillpott asked.

Kitty shrugged, but Myles set his jaw.

"Trust me, it was deserved."

Phillpot glared at Myles. "May I have a word with you, alone?"

Myles nodded, but Kitty stood her ground, wary.

"Go along, Kitty. I am sure, I can handle Mr. Philpott if he requires further discipline."

Kitty nodded before leaving the study, and silence followed the swish of her skirts.

"What do you want, Philpott?" Myles was in no mood to give the man any quarter. He didn't deserve it after the history Myles had learned of Charlotte's family.

Philpott frowned. "I've come to collect Charlotte."

"She's not a thing. Charlotte is a woman who can make her own choices," Myles said defensively.

"She does not seem to be making wise choices. Even though I was misinformed about who exactly is in residence here, she still should not be here alone."

"Your sister arrived at Mosswin with Miss Kendall. I hardly think Lady Devonhold would send her sister to a house rife with scandal."

"Regardless, Charlotte sent word to me, and I traveled across England to bloody Scotland to arrive at your doorstep, hoping to find my sister safe and hale, and yet she has once again eluded me." Philpott rubbed his temples as if the entire process pained him.

"She may not want to leave with you. Since you left her to her own devices, we—"

"Yes, yes! She wrote to me about her plan. Forgive me if I do not want to see her installed as a mistress. Regardless of how good you may be to her, she deserves something more respectable," Philpott growled.

He frowned. "She's *not* my mistress. You darken my doorstep because you are worried about a scandal, rather than your sister's well-being?"

Philpott raised an eyebrow. "I came to see my sister home safely, to *my* home. If she is not your mistress, why is she still in residence?"

Though he didn't want to reveal Charlotte's ridiculous handfasting idea, he would tell her brother the truth. "Charlotte is my wife."

Philpott's surprise gave way to a wide smile. "Wife? Well, then, a marriage is different."

Charlotte's voice rang through the open doorway.

"What are you doing here, Nigel?"

Both men turned to find. Charlotte, Miss Kendall, and his mother were staring at them from the hall, while. Kitty lingered behind them, still armed with her cane.

Charlotte couldn't believe her ears. They discussed her situation without her present, as though she were a child. Did she matter so little to her brother, once he'd learned now that she was properly married, that he could simply smile and say all was well? The crushing weight of the past surged forward, and her parents' faces swam before her eyes. This was why she'd married Robert because she'd wanted to make her own decisions regardless of how wrong they had been.

"My dearest Charlotte." Nigel crossed the room to enfold her in his arms. "I've been worried sick about you."

She shook free of his hold and backed away, suspicious. When had he changed? Why? "Not enough to fetch me after Robert died."

"I am sorry. My travel plans had already been made."

She threw her hands up. "Of course. Your trip was more important than my husband's funeral. More important than my grief! More important than *me*! The only people who came to his memorial were

Amelia and her family." She knew she sounded petulant, but she didn't care. Her brother's concern came too late and with no substance.

Nigel stared off into the distance as if she hadn't spoken.

Charlotte set her heels and raised her chin. "I am not going with you."

"There is no need, now that you are a wife," Nigel cooed.

Infuriated by Nigel's bland acquiescence, Charlotte erupted. "Now he speaks! You have no use for me. Your curiosity and concern for the family's reputation have been satisfied, so you may leave." She gave him her back.

Nigel touched her shoulder. "Now, Charlotte—"

Turning, she threw his hand aside. "No, Nigel, you have no say in my life. I have been under the thumb of more than one man. First our Father and then Robert."

Her brother ran his hands through his hair. "And what about Major Ashton?"

Charlotte balled her hands into fists, fighting the temptation to hit him. "He is different. At least here I have found a place where I belong, and no! I am done talking with you! You've assured yourself of my safety and well-being, for what it's worth, and now I am taking my leave. I suggest you do the same." She turned to flee, but the doorway was filled with the stunned faces of her new family. Finding herself trapped, her breath hitched, and she tripped. The floor rushed upward but Myles caught her.

"Thank you," she choked. Charlotte raised her eyes to find Myles watching her.

"Always." The concern in her husband's expression was mixed with confusion.

Heat crawled along her neck. She owed everyone an apology, but the look in Myles' eyes rendered her speechless. She leaned into Myles for support as he steadied her on her feet.

A servant caught Lady Mosswin's attention in the hallway, and Charlotte used the opportunity to escape. She broke free of Ashton's hold, pushed past the ladies in the hallway, and ran as fast as she could to her room upstairs.

The sound of footsteps followed her, but she knew who it was before she turned.

Myles stared at her, his brow furrowed. "Are you all right?"

"I'll be fine. I need a few minutes to myself."

"Take your time. If you want, I can send dinner up."

"No, I am not sure if this feeling of..." What was she feeling?

"Boldness?" he supplied.

She smiled at his reference to what her brother and others might call recklessness, but not her husband, no he didn't seem to mind the barbs in her personality. "Yes, boldness. I shall recover by supper." With any luck, by then her brother would have left for his decadent pursuits.

Charlotte had never been lucky. Ever the courteous hostess, Lady Mosswin invited Nigel to dinner, and Her brother stayed for several days. Although they remained cordial, they did not speak until the day he readied to leave.

Nigel tracked her to the stables, where the groom prepared her horse for a ride. "Charlotte, a word?"

"Certainly. Would you care to join me?" At least if he irritated her, she could outpace and outsmart him. Her brother did not sit a horse well.

"I think not. This will be rather brief. I am leaving today."

"Oh, well, goodbye." She turned back to her horse.

"Please walk with me." For all Nigel's grace and sincerity, it was a command, nonetheless. The look on his face was deadly serious and his feet were planted.

Charlotte sighed. She recognized the look of stubbornness. Nigel would stand until his feet grew roots. She might as well listen to whatever he needed to say so she could bid him adieu. She extended her hand for him to lead the way.

Nigel led her past the stables to the rose garden at the back of the house.

Charlotte quickened her step to keep up with his longer stride. "What do you have to say?"

Her brother smiled. "No beating around the bush, eh?"

"No. I have been quiet and meek for far too long." Charlotte smiled inwardly. Myles had given her a newfound pride, which bolstered her courage.

"You had little choice, as a child," Nigel murmured. "I am glad to see you well. This place," he gestured to their surroundings, "seems to agree with you."

"It does."

"Look, Charlee..."

Her eyes misted as he used the name he'd called her when they were children. She was three years his senior. When he was younger, he'd taken to calling her Charlee. She longed to hold him and capture some of what they lost. Instead, she stopped and stared at him. Though he gave the impression he was carefree with his golden hair and gray eyes, he was hardened, too, as if something lay beneath the surface wanting freedom.

"I am sorry. I didn't mean to muck up your life. I wanted to let you know I will not reveal your whereabouts to our parents."

"Do you still see them?" She was curious how his relationship fared after she left.

"Only if I must, which is blessedly rare," Nigel sighed, looking forlorn.

"You are always welcome here." She was certain Ashton wouldn't mind.

"I may return. You seem happy with this husband."

If not a loving marriage like Amelia's, she believed her relationship with Myles would be an honest one, and not the dire life sentence she once believed. "I am. It seems fate was kinder this time."

"It is a shame he is only a Lord. You could have done better."

Charlotte was so taken aback by this sudden criticism that she nearly missed his smirk. She punched him in the shoulder. "You rat. Before I caught you smiling, I was worried that you had spent too much time with our aspiring mother."

Nigel rubbed his arm and chuckled. "After spending a few days at Mosswin, I see why you are happy. This recent and haphazardly assembled branch of the Fitzwilliam family seems to have a sense of honor and no-nonsense which, well... after our upbringing, I can understand the appeal of finally finding a home."

Home. Charlotte hadn't given it much thought but now that Nigel mentioned it, Mosswin *did* feel like home. She'd grown fond of Kitty. Even Lady Mosswin was less abrasive and more amiable of late. And then there was Myles. She loved Myles. The realization landed in her gut and caused her to stumble.

Nigel caught her. "Are you feeling ill?"

"Oh. Yes— no, I am fine."

"I can call for someone." His brow wrinkled and his eyes scanned her.

"No." Suddenly Charlotte didn't want her brother to leave. "Must you go?" Mosswin held a special magic to mend broken things, including her.

"I am afraid I must. I feel as though I am a bit underfoot. But do not fret. I have something for you." Nigel reached into his pocket and handed her a key.

"What is this?" she asked.

"A key to my townhouse in Russell Square."

"A key?"

"Should you ever need it, I'll let the staff know you are welcome. Although I suspect you shall not return to London anytime soon."

Charlotte shook her head. She would remain at Mosswin. She was astonished at the fulfillment in her heart. It was an awakening moment. It seemed as though Myles and Mosswin had captured her very soul.

Chapter Seventeen

The hour Nigel Philpott had departed that afternoon, Myles' family arrived en masse. They must have passed each other on the road. Myles stood in the door, his plans for Charlotte crashing about his ears. As he watched his cousin, Lady Worthington, appear in the door of her carriage, he gave thanks that his mother had accepted Philpott's offer of escort to London so that she and Kitty could visit the London modistes.

"What are you doing here?" Myles asked as the group exited their carriages and bordered alongside his front steps. *Dear Lord!* Where was he going to place all of them? His panic only slightly subsided when he noticed Amelia's sisters were absent.

"Why, we've come to see your new home, cousin," Lady Worthington gestured to the manor as if their arrival was most obvious.

"We received word from Errington as to your true parentage," James clarified while helping his wife descend the carriage. Amelia showed signs of increasing since he'd last seen her.

"Is it safe for you to travel?" Myles asked.

"I am fine." Amelia's eyes scanned the doorway. "Is Arabella about?"

"I am afraid not. She left with Mr. Philpott not an hour past for London."

"Oh? Did Charlotte go as well?" Amelia pressed a hand to her abdomen.

"No, I am present," Charlotte said from behind him.

Myles had been so taken aback by the arrival of his 'family' that he'd forgotten she had been in his mother's garden of roses. He'd had plans for her today, blast it! Plans which were rudely interrupted.

Amelia pursed her lips. "It doesn't seem appropriate for Arabella to travel with Nigel, regardless of how nice your brother is."

"Do not worry about your sister's reputation. Lady Mosswin and Ashton's sister, Kitty, went with them." Charlotte assured her.

"To what end?"

"My mother is buying my sister a travel wardrobe for her glorious adventure," Myles clarified without preamble.

"A glorious adventure? What is that?" Amelia tilted her head to the side.

Charlotte was the first to answer. "It's a bit like a grand tour, only for bold—"

"—and adventurous," Myles interjected.

"... bold and adventurous young women," Charlotte finished, giving him a winsome smile.

Damn! Why had his family shown up the very day he finally had Charlotte to himself?

"I've never heard of anything so preposterous. Can you imagine, James?" Joan said in mock shock.

Myles suspected she was perhaps a bit jealous that she'd never had an adventure. "You will find we are a bit unconventional on this side of the family," Myles supplied. He wasn't about to let her belittle the decision he and his mother made regarding Kitty's education.

"Touché," James said, smiling.

"Well, Ashton, do not stand about dawdling. Have your servants get us settled," Joan demanded.

"Myles," he corrected her.

"I beg your pardon."

"I prefer you call me Myles." He was done suffering insults from his petulant cousin.

His family fell silent.

"Myles. I always did like that name," Amelia spoke up.

Charlotte took over with ease. "Then let us see you settled. Rogers, see to their comfort." She installed Joan in Kitty's room and situated Amelia and James in his mother's.

He dared not imagine what his mother would think if the snobbish Lady Worthington had access to her bedroom.

After the drama of room assignments concluded, Myles searched for Charlotte, but she had slipped away. He was breathing heavily with each step and near exhaustion when he finally found her. She'd returned to the rose garden and was seated on a rose-etched bench, set against the backdrop of the roses themselves.

"How can you suffer in this place?"

"What do you mean?" Charlotte asked.

"The roses." Myles gestured towards the offensive buds, a few beginning their pinkish bloom.

"You do not like roses?" Her gentle laughter rippled through the air.

He found himself smiling in response. "Not when I find myself drowning in them. Mother has them everywhere, even on the walls."

"They are special to her."

"I didn't come here to converse about the flora." He tried to sound serious since they were about to discuss their future.

She gave him a small smile, letting him know he failed. "Why did you desire to speak with me?"

"Will you join me?" He offered his arm, and Charlotte accepted. She accepted. "Of course."

His mother arranged to leave with Kitty and Arabella after Philpott was gone so Myles could be alone with Charlotte. Myles led Charlotte away from the garden, toward the old castle ruins, grateful for his mother's succor. His mother had taken his sister to London so he could finally reveal his plans to Charlotte. But when his 'family' arrived, he was thrown off balance, and now he struggled to remember his words.

They arrived far too quickly at the ruins, and Myles' well-rehearsed speech went awry. He blurted his next words. "I am giving you Mosswin Castle."

Charlotte's mouth fell open and she clutched his arm so she would not fall. "You're giving me this castle."

Myles raised his chin. "Yes."

"But... it's unfinished," she said, puzzled as to what she would do with the building in ruins.

"I'll begin repairs in the summer," he said, his voice and gaze strong.

"Why?"

"Mosswin Castle is my wedding gift to you."

"Oh, Myles!" Tears threatened to fall, and she struggled to hold them in check.

"What is wrong?" Myles wiped a drop from her cheek with the pad of his thumb.

"Nothing, you fool. I love you. I want to be with you, and more importantly, I trust you," she confessed.

"You do?" He regarded her with something akin to awe. "I hadn't expected to win your heart so quickly."

Myles skimmed his fingers over her jawline. "I do not want to ruin this moment."

Heart pounding, she took a quick breath. "Speaking of ruins, why are you giving me this castle?"

"I thought we could make a school of the finished building. A school for girls like Kitty."

"You are giving me a school?"

"No...yes... Charlotte, I love you. I want to give you the world, but for now, you must settle for this castle in dire need of repairs." His hand dropped to his side.

"Finished or not. I accept your generous gift." This man was gifting her with her heart's desire. The building wasn't as important as his gesture, or him.

"It will be our house as well," Myles murmured. "You will be headmistress and determine the curriculum for bold and adventurous girls."

"Daring debutantes."

"Precisely," he agreed with a grin.

She could resist temptation no longer and threw herself into his arms. "You have made me the happiest of women."

"I would not be here without you." Myles smiled.

"You are the heir, regardless of me. You'd have arrived here eventually on your own." Charlotte lowered her gaze, hiding beneath her eyelashes.

"But I wouldn't have been nearly as satisfied."

Myles pressed his hips against hers, and she folded her arms around his neck. "You find me satisfying, do you?"

"In all ways. I cannot imagine my life without you." He bent his head forward, and his breath caressed her cheek.

"Nor me without you. I love you too." Charlotte let his lips slide over hers. She regretted the time spent without him through her foolishness. At last, she had a home with a man she loved. It was everything she'd hoped for, but Myles was all she truly needed.

Myles led her to the ruins, where he had laid a blanket on the grass. Pillows and a picnic basket made the rustic scene almost civil. He proceeded to show her all the ways they were complete together.

Epilogue

September 29th, 1816
Michaelmas

Charlotte couldn't believe how well the castle was coming together. Exhausted, she drew the curtains closed, shutting out the growing darkness, and collapsed on the bed.

Ashton stood nearby, removing his jacket. "We aren't quite done with the day."

"Oh? Is there something I am forgetting, Laird Ashton?"

"Minx. You know I've barely been able to keep my hands off you. And my family wasn't helping, milling sociably about the dining room after dinner."

Reluctantly, she stood and gave him innocent eyes while presenting him with her back. "Put your hands to work, then, or I'll have to call the maid to undo my buttons."

Ashton began undoing the rows of buttons on her silver dress. His mother had selected the material from the modiste, and Amelia claimed the silver lamé dress brought a sparkle to Charlotte's eyes.

As Myles undid each button, he placed a lingering, tantalizing kiss on the exposed skin of her neck.

Charlotte shivered in anticipation.

Finally, with enough buttons undone, Myles slid the gown over her hips, leaving it in a puddle at her feet. She stepped from the silver fabric, kicking off her kid slippers as she did so. She stood before him in her chemise and stockings.

When she turned to look at her husband, he was still mostly dressed. He'd removed his shirt, but he remained in his trousers.

"I am feeling a bit exposed," she said.

Myles drew her into his arms, his large hands gently holding her face. He bent his head, his tongue traced the soft fullness of her lips.

She parted them, and he explored her mouth slowly and thoughtfully.

Charlotte's body ached for him, so she wound her arms around his neck and buried her face in his throat, nipping at his flesh.

"Are we impatient, wife?" he growled.

She gave him a siren's smile. "As if you didn't know that already, with all the kisses you've granted on my person this day."

Myles swung her up into the circle of his arms, carrying her to the bed, where he set her on the edge. His gaze was bold, the heat of it racing through her. "Are you ready for me?"

"Yes," she answered, honestly. When it came to Ashton, she was in a perpetual state of want. His family's arrival for Michaelmas and an inspection of the repairs done to the castle had given rise to stolen glances and brief kisses.

Myles lightly traced a path along the soft lines of her waist and hips, exploring and arousing her. His palm caressed the skin of her thigh, burning into her tingling skin. A single finger lightly tested her folds, wet and waiting. "Very ready indeed."

When he positioned his manhood at her entrance and pressed forward, Charlotte released a moan at the welcome intrusion. She felt the heady sensation of his lips on her neck as he whispered how beautiful and passionate she was, and his pace became primal and rhythmic. She had a burning desire, an aching need to press her lips to his. She drew his face to hers in a renewed embrace.

Their lips met and she was buffeted by savage harmony. Ashton continued thrusting into her until her climax reached a crescendo and she cried out.

"I am right behind you, wife," Myles gasped. A few more thrusts and he went over as well.

They both collapsed on the bed.

"Ashton, I have a present for you."

"Was that not my present?" Myles smiled.

"No. Well, yes, but I shall have another for you in about seven months."

He leaned on his elbow, resting his head on his hand. "We are going to have a baby?"

"Yes."

"So, you're not barren. The late Reverend was...."

"Unable to grant me children, but you will." She smiled at the irony. She would have the family she wanted and with her perfect husband, no less.

Ashton pulled her to him, nearly crushing her. "I love you."

"And I love you. We shall have to think of some baby names."

"Would you mind Edgar if it's a boy?"

"Not at all, as long as you do not mind if I pick our daughter's name."

"What did you have in mind?"

"How about…" She couldn't resist teasing him. "Rose?"

He cringed. "Absolutely, not."

"Too bad! I like the name, and you will learn to as well."

"I guarantee if we have a girl named Rose I won't like it."

"You won't?" Charlotte bit her lip.

"No. I will love her, as I love her mother."

And he did.

Letter to my Readers

Dear Readers,

I hope you enjoyed *How to Marry a Major*. Feel free to leave a review at your favorite site for others. I would greatly appreciate it.

I wanted to note that while *Canne de Combat* originated in the early 19th Century in France, it may or may not have been familiar to an English soldier in the Regency period. However, I wanted to give Kitty every tool she needed for her future.

I've included an excerpt of Book Two in the **Bold and Adventurous Debutante's Guide** series, *How to Love a Lord,* featuring Arabella and Pierce, in the following pages, for your pleasure.

Feel free to follow me on social media. All my links can be found on my website. You can also sign up for my newsletter there. I only email regarding upcoming releases or deals my publishers are running.

Thanks again for purchasing this book. Your patronage is appreciated.

Tina Holland

My Fair Lord

Following a night of passion where she is mistaken for her twin, Arabella Kendall resolves to never tell anyone, especially Pierce, the man who claimed her. With her sister Amelia, insisting on a season, Arabella agrees it's time to search for a husband, even if she must reveal her torrid past.

Pierce Ellis, Viscount Kernwith has only ever loved one woman, Amelia Fitzwilliam, the countess of Devonhold, or so he thought. When he discovers it was Arabella all along, he wonders how he could have been wrong and immediately wants to correct the matter.

As Pierce pursues Arabella, he must also save Kernwith from ruin. Together they uncover the secrets of his estate. Will Arabella give her heart to Pierce or never forgive him for the past?

Excerpt

Pierce Ellis, Viscount of Kernwith waited by the punch bowl. He was in no hurry to bring back beverages. Frankly, he didn't think the widow or Major Ashton would notice. And for whatever reason, Arabella Kendall was downright combative. When he looked back no one stood where they had been. He shrugged. It was just as well.

Maybe Amelia had told Arabella what had transpired between them. The ladies were twins, and they likely shared secrets. Pierce didn't understand the dynamics of siblings, but perhaps Arabella held a grudge on behalf of her sister.

He watched as Amelia departed the dance floor with her husband. Why had he agreed to come to Devonhold? It was obvious Amelia had moved on when she married Fitzwilliam. She'd likely invited him because he was now a noble, and she was looking to pair the eligible ladies, or maybe just her siblings and Charlotte Wold.

Across the room, Lord Devonhold abandoned his bride and greeted Lord Worthington and the other cronies. Cronies the former Lord

Kernwith knew. No one would welcome him — an outsider of the peerage.

His heart pounded as Amelia approached him. A siren's smile crossed her features. His thoughts scrambled as he remembered the last time he was with this woman.

"I hope you are having a good time," she said.

"To be honest, I was surprised to receive an invitation." Did she hear the bitterness in his voice? Did she care?

She lightly slapped his arm with her fan. "Poppycock! We are neighbors now. You are always welcome here."

"Am I?" What did she expect of him?

"Of course. James isn't a snob." She waved across the room at her husband.

Lord Devonhold nodded.

His gut tightened and he knew he would never be comfortable in the presence of her and her loving husband. "Why did you marry him?" .

Amelia didn't even acknowledge him, her eyes still on Devonhold. "I love him, of course."

He was flabbergasted. "You love him?! The last time we saw each other, you told me you would not marry him."

She didn't spare him a glance. "My lord, that was not me."

"Obviously." He took a step back wanting distance between them. Who was this woman who clawed at his heart?

Finally, she turned. "You misunderstand. I sent Arabella to meet with you."

"What? Impossible. She... We... I mean... I would've known." He backed into a column and leaned against it. His stomach clenched as the room spun.

She frowned at him. "Whenever you sent those silly notes to meet you, I usually sent Arabella. Honestly, I don't even know why you were interested. It's not as if we knew each other before your father invited us to Kernwith."

When he didn't answer, she continued. "I know I should not have let you maintain your interest, but until I met James, I didn't know what love was. I hope you understand." She patted his arm again. Suddenly, her touch felt foreign and cold. He didn't feel the same quickening as before.

"Of course." He turned away from her, wanting to escape, but something stopped him. "Wait!"

She tilted her head to the side. "Yes?"

"When did we first meet?"

Her delicate blond brow arched. "An odd question."

"When, Amelia?!"

Her features became more animated. "We met when your father hosted the country party last summer. It was before I met James," she sighed. "I think I knew even then James and I would be together."

"The first evening, when you came to the stables during the dance?" he clarified.

"No. It was on the hunt the following day. Are you feeling alright, Lord Kernwith?"

"Fine, fine." He needed to get away from her, and fate granted him an unlikely ally.

"Ah, here comes my wonderful lord." With a quick twirl, she turned away from Pierce to greet her husband.

Was it always Arabella? Had he stupidly fallen in love with the wrong woman, or worse, both? He scanned the room looking for Arabella, but she seemed to have vanished.

Devonhold greeted him. "Good to see you, Ellis."

"You too. If you will excuse me." Unable to bear their nauseatingly happy presence, he wandered the edge of the ballroom before settling against the door frame outside the cardroom.

There sat Arabella, playing cards with her twin, the Widow Wold, and Lady Worthington. He looked at her, really looked at her. How did he not know? Why hadn't she told him? He couldn't help but stare at her. As if she sensed his scrutiny, she looked up and met his gaze with her illuminated green eyes. A frown crossed her features before she lowered her head. He now understood her ire since the wedding. She had every chance to correct him since that day and should have. Well, he would correct the matter now. Before he could step foot into the room he was halted.

"Kernwith!"

Startled, Pierce turned to find Major Ashton marching toward him. "Ashton, what do you want?"

"Have a drink with me."

Pierce eyed him suspiciously. "Why?"

"Because a man shouldn't wallow alone."

Pierce nodded. He could use a drink. Some liquid courage before he confronted Arabella about her deception.

Milton Keynes UK
Ingram Content Group UK Ltd.
UKHW040312080224
437360UK00001B/48